Books & Bullets

Cameron Hart

Published by Cameron Hart, 2024.

BOOKS & BULLETS

First edition. February 23, 2024.

ISBN: 979-8227068613

Written by Cameron Hart.

Want a free book?

Sign up for my newsletter[1] and get your free copy of Chasing Stacy!

One look at the stunning waitress carrying the weight of the world on her shoulders, and I'm a goner. I wasn't looking for a sweet little thing with auburn hair and more baggage than I can fit on the back of my bike, but there's no going back now. She's mine. I'll prove to her I'm more than capable of handling her past and making her feel safe again.

---

1. https://dl.bookfunnel.com/7wbqvhsx8r

Connect with me!

Check out my website, cameronhart.net[2], for sneak previews on my latest projects.

Follow me on social media:

Facebook Page - facebook.com/cameronhartauthor
Instagram - instagram.com/cameron.hart.author
TikTok - tiktok.com/@author.cameron.hart
Goodreads - goodreads.com/16081533.Cameron_Hart
Bookbub - bookbub.com/authors/cameron-hart

Chapter 1

Slater

I slam my fist into the punching bag with enough force to rattle the frame. It's still not enough. I throw punches left and right, pummeling the leather, sand-filled bag until my hands throb and sweat pours down my face and neck.

My muscles ache from my impromptu midnight boxing session, but I can't stop. Not when I'm this worked up. Not when I still hear the tortured cries of my fallen brothers and sisters. Not when I still see the carnage left in the wake of that damn roadside bomb.

Will the nightmares ever stop? Will I always be haunted by the souls of those I left behind? Questions race through my mind as I work out my frustration one blow at a time.

I keep going, leaning into the pain, punishing myself for surviving when so many others died. My shoulder protests with each movement, a poignant reminder that although I lived, I didn't come out unscathed.

When the humvee ran over the roadside bomb and flew in the air before rolling six times, I knew I was dead. The impact somehow launched my six-foot-eleven frame through the back of the vehicle, and I landed a solid fifteen feet away from the crash. I watched in stunned horror as the massive humvee erupted into flames.

"Fuck," I curse, gritting my teeth and sinking my fist into the punching bag once more.

I remember pulling myself up off the desert floor, only to collapse a few feet later. My collar bone had snapped, my left femur was crushed, and I had more broken ribs than not. Still, I clawed my way through the sand, needing to save my fellow soldiers.

A surreal flashback clouds my vision and I cough as my nostrils fill with the smell of smoke and burning flesh. It's so real. I can feel the heat of the fire on my face and arms as I drag my body across the sand and dirt. Just like every flashback and nightmare, I never make it in time.

The entire scene explodes in my mind, just like it did in real life, and then blackness greets me.

My leg spasms at the memory, and I snap back into the present. Stumbling forward, I catch myself on the swinging punching bag. Breathless and broken, I decide to wash up and start the day.

It's only four-thirty in the morning, but I'm wide awake. It's unusual for me to sleep past four these days. Most nights, my visceral nightmares tear me apart until I jerk awake, alone and panicking in the dark. There's no going to bed after that. I'm lucky to get four hours of sleep a night.

I slide into the shower, letting the scalding water burn away the last of the flashback clinging to me. As I wash up, my hands linger on the jagged scars littering my body. A spiderweb of raised skin spreads across my right thigh from where the bone broke through, and the multiple surgeries it took to fix. My left shoulder also bears angry scars from broken bones and surgery. A discolored, ugly patch of flesh stretches across my right side, up my rib cage. Between the burns and broken bones, I had to get a skin graft to heal properly.

My fingers trace the disfigured skin as I wash the soap away. I came back from the military ugly and scared in more ways than one. The guilt eats away at me every day, the anger, the unfairness of it all. Sometimes, I worry I'll wake up and have nothing left. Just emptiness and a shriveled up soul.

I shut the shower off and shake the water out of my hair, along with my morose thoughts. At least I have a job to keep me busy most days. The long nights and early mornings alone with my thoughts are rough, but being part owner of Watchdog Protection, Inc., has given me a purpose and a distraction.

My military buddies, Logan and Colton, got out a few years before I did. I would have made the Marines my career if not for that goddamn bomb that splintered my life apart.

There were some dark days, hell there still are plenty of dark days, but Logan and Colton got me through the worst of it. The stubborn bastards stayed by my side during countless surgeries and the subsequent recovery time.

It was their idea to use our skills as ex-Marines to form a security company. I wanted no part in it at first. I failed to protect my unit, so how could I offer protection to someone else? Plus, it's not like I'm at the top of my game, physically speaking.

Yes, I go a few rounds with the punching bag most days, and I can still run, jump, and shoot a gun just fine. But I'm not at my peak. It's not my best and I get sore and tired more easily than I used to, though part of that might just be from getting older. At thirty six, I'm not ancient, but I feel like I've lived several lives worth of suffering. It shows in my eyes, my face, and my weathered hands.

After throwing on jeans and a black t-shirt, I brew some strong-ass coffee. Black as mud and just as thick. Years of drinking the motor oil provided by the military grew on me, and now I like my coffee this way. Maybe it's the bitter taste that so often goes with my mood or maybe it's just the routine of sipping a shitty cup of caffeine. Either way, once I'm done, I rinse out the mug and finally head out the door.

My house is as far away from the city as I could manage while still being able to get to the Watchdog offices in downtown Chicago. The plot of land isn't big, but it serves its purpose. I don't need anything fancy, and it's not like I have anyone to impress. As long as I have space to work out and work on my clay projects, I'm fine.

No one else knows about the other thing that keeps me somewhat sane. I box and push my body to the limit when I'm amped up, but when I'm drowning in emotions I can't process, I head down to my studio. Feeling the cold clay bend and mold to my touch soothes the gnawing ache in my chest little by little. Having the power to create or the power to destroy, gives me some sort of control over my life. At least, while I'm in the studio.

Pulling into the office, I park my SUV and step out, stretching after being cramped up for the fifteen-minute drive. My truck is tall and wide, much like me, but I still have to fold my nearly seven-foot self into the cab.

"Slater," Colton greets me when I walk inside. "How's it going?"

I nod my head once, letting him know I'm good. Or, well, good for me. The bar is set pretty low.

"Did Logan tell you about your new assignment before he went off to Cali?" he continues, unfazed by my silence. I don't use my words too much these days, but Logan and Colton have learned to translate my silent nods and occasional grunts.

I catch his eye and frown, shaking my head no. Logan was supposed to be here today to tell me, but I woke up to a text saying he's out of town.

"I figured," Colton sighs. "He wanted me to be the bearer of bad news, I guess," he says half-jokingly.

Furrowing my brow, I tilt my head to the side, wanting him to continue. I'm fine with any assignment as long as it gets me out of my house and out of my head. If I spend too long in either place, the darkness threatens to consume me.

"It's at a rinky-dink library," Colton says. "There have been reports of an unidentified man lurking around the place. Last week, they suspected he broke in. Nothing was stolen, but things were messy and out of place when the head librarian came in to open for the day. Yesterday, he tripped the alarm right as the library was closing. Luckily, there were only two people inside, both employees, and they got away before calling the cops."

I nod, taking in all the information. Guarding the library against some nerd who wants to break in sounds easy enough, but that's not the part troubling me. It sounds like I'll have a lot of free time just hanging out in the library, waiting for some action. Free time means my thoughts have the chance to run wild.

"It's just for a few weeks," Colton says, a slight pleading edge to his tone. "I'm still wrapping things up with my last assignment and Logan is out in California getting into trouble. I have a feeling the girl he's supposed to protect is more than he bargained for." I know he just wants a rise out of me, so I shrug my shoulder. "Yup, Logan has his hands full with that girl. Wouldn't be surprised if he came back with a ring on his finger."

Colton chuckles and I roll my eyes. The charming cowboy has always believed love would cure Logan's orderly life and my darkness. I think he should shut up and find love for himself instead of bugging us about it.

I wipe a hand down my face as I think about hanging out at the library for eight hours a day. Three years ago, I was seeing action. I can still feel the cool metal of my sniper rifle, still smell the acrid gun smoke when I popped off a shot. Now, I'm being sent to walk around a library and look out for suspicious characters, all while having a silent battle in my mind.

"You okay, man?" Colton asks, rubbing the back of his neck. I know he's not just asking about my new assignment. It's still awkward as fuck to talk about my time in the military. At least Colton and Logan have some kind of understanding of what I've been through.

"Rough morning," I grunt, clearing my throat. He knows exactly what I mean without me having to elaborate.

"Up early hitting the bag again?"

"Gotta stay in shape," I reply. We both know I punch the shit out of the bag because I can't fight my real demons, but neither of us mentions that.

Logan calls a few minutes later to give me the details of the job and to check on the offices. All three of us own Watchdog, but Logan is the one with the head for business. The guy is ultra-organized and detail-oriented. He's got lists on lists of tasks, reminders, and who knows what else. He says it keeps him sane, and who am I to judge?

"Here you go, sunshine!" Colton says once I've hung up with Logan. He gives me a bright smile before handing me a folder with a library map as well as a dossier about the library employees.

Skimming over names and headshots, my eyes snag on one entry in particular. Raven Markus. The picture is black and white, but her beauty radiates through the paper. Her dark hair is pulled into a tight bun, revealing her slender neck. Allowing my gaze to travel upward, her perfect cupid's bow lips taunt me, begging me to kiss them.

The photo shakes, and I realize I'm trembling. My breath comes out in short pants and my heart stills then races into overdrive.

I rub the heel of my hand over my chest, unsure where the sudden jolt of energy and tension came from. I haven't been with a woman... fuck, in ten years? No, closer to fifteen. That has to be why I'm obsessing over lips, for fuck's sake.

Trailing my eyes over the photo, I take in her nose, slightly turned up at the end in the most adorable way. Black, sooty eyelashes frame her gorgeous eyes. Since the picture is black and white, I can't tell what color they are. However, I know they're just as captivating as the rest of her.

"Slater?" Colton asks, his voice cutting through my confusing lust. "Do you want to switch assignments?"

"No," I say harshly. My meaty paw tightens around the paper I'm holding, crushing it in a possessive grip. Colton looks at me with wide eyes, but I shrug him off. I need to know what it is about this girl. I need to see more than just a headshot. I need the whole damn picture.

Chapter 2

Giving myself one last look in the mirror, I straighten my cardigan and clasp the top button closed. I tuck a stray hair back into my bun, looping it around the stretchy hair tie to secure it in place.

Looking at my phone, I see it's eight-fifty. Perfect. It takes me exactly ten minutes to walk from my studio apartment to my job at the library. I don't have to be there until closer to nine-thirty, but I like getting there early and taking my time to get everything ready before the doors open at ten.

I double-check my backpack to make sure I packed my lunch, then square my shoulders, preparing to head out for the day. Glancing through the peephole, I make sure no one else is out there before undoing the three locks on my door and step outside.

My eyes instinctively dart to the left and right, and I'm keenly aware of my surroundings as I lock everything back up and turn around. *Stop looking so suspicious!* the voice in my head whisper-shouts.

Easier said than done when there are powerful men after you who want to force you into a life you never asked for. An image of my dad's gray eyes turning black flashes through my mind. I knew he was an important businessman with more money than God, but I didn't understand the sacrifices it took to get him there and the price he still had to pay.

My father and I were never particularly close. After my mom left him for some young pro-surfer when I was ten, he pretty much checked out of parenthood. I can't complain, though. The staff around our estate raised me the best they knew how. I always had plenty to eat, the most fashionable clothes to wear, and the best education money could buy. So what if I didn't get hugs or goodnight kisses? I have a lot to be thankful for.

Or, I did. Silly me. Everything comes at a cost. Dear old Dad didn't teach me much, but he drilled that lesson home. I wasn't ready to pay the price he asked, so I ran. Hopped on a bus, then hitchhiked for a stretch before catching another bus to Chicago.

I clear my head and take a deep breath, hiking my backpack up a little higher on my shoulder as I walk toward the library.

I've been in Chicago for six months now. When I first arrived, I stayed in a fleabag motel and scoped out my living options with what little cash I had left. I never had to budget or make money stretch to the end of the month, but I quickly learned that survival skill.

I come to a stop at a crosswalk, wrapping my arms around myself tightly as I wait for the light to change. It's an instinct now to make myself as small as possible, to be invisible. I get uncomfortable when I'm just standing still like there's a target on me. If I can keep moving, keep pushing through, keep my head down and live a normal life, everything will be fine. My dad will have to stop looking for me eventually. Right?

God, I hope so.

The traffic comes to a stop and the crosswalk flashes, giving me the go-ahead to cross the busy intersection. I scurry across the street, nearly tripping when I reach the other side. *Real smooth*, I berate myself as I catch my breath. For someone trying to go around unnoticed, I'm awfully clumsy. If I'm not tripping over something, my wide hips are knocking things off tables.

Gathering my wits about me, I turn the corner and finally see the library. My sanctuary. Getting hired on as an assistant librarian was the best thing to happen in all my twenty years.

Books have always been an escape for me. Diving into dangerous adventures, passionate love stories, and heart-wrenching tragedies was my favorite pastime growing up. It still is. So getting to handle these precious stories every day and help others find worlds to get lost in is pretty much a dream come true.

When I'm within the book-covered walls of the library, nothing can touch me. I'm not running from evil men with evil plans. I'm not living on a shoestring budget in a tiny apartment. I'm not shy and awkward and lonely. Between the pages of a book, I can be anyone, and sometimes, that's just what I need.

I dig around in my backpack for the keys to open the door, shuffling my way through the parking lot to get to the back entrance. Pulling the keys out of my bag, I look up and freeze.

A giant man is standing off to the left, partially hidden in the shadow of the overhang. His back is turned to me, those broad shoulders taking up nearly my entire view.

Shit! Did my father send him? He's huge!

I start to back away from the door, but my foot catches on the uneven pavement. My arms pinwheel around me as I swallow down a gasp. My ballerina flats scrape across the asphalt and I drop the keys, which jangle and bounce on the ground.

"*Oom*ph," I grunt as I hit the cement, one shoe flying off in the process.

I'm about to scramble up and run for my life, but the man turns his enormous frame toward me, locking his gaze onto mine.

Blue.

So blue.

Pure, deep, overwhelming blue eyes bore right into my freaking soul as he stares at me. A spark of recognition flickers across his face, which only confirms my suspicions. My father must have shown him my photo when he sent the man to collect me.

"I... I'm..." I choke on my next breath, sputtering as I hold his intense gaze. I can't look away. Not when he's digging around in my heart and making me feel things I can't even begin to explain.

The tall, dark stranger takes a step forward and I flinch, fighting back tears.

He stops suddenly, those blue eyes filling with shock and then... concern?

I watch in awe, totally frozen in place, as the man kneels in front of me. My heart riots in my chest, my skin tingles and heats up, and still, I can't tear my eyes away from him.

He slowly reaches for my shoe, his eyes never leaving mine as he grabs it and slips it onto my foot. I'm shaking and confused when the man puts his hands in front of him, palms up as if to show me he's no threat. Something changes in his gaze, softening his rough edges and hard angles.

"Are you okay?" he rasps out, wincing at his own harsh tone. I open my mouth to say... *something*, but I have no words. If he's going to kidnap me, why does he care? And if he wasn't sent here by my father, then what is he doing here? The man reaches out for me and I scramble backward on instinct. "Shit, sorry," he mutters, dropping his hand.

I jump up with a sudden burst of energy, only to stumble forward. My head is spinning from my shallow breathing, but I manage to stay upright. Blinking one eye open and then the other, I get my first good look at the lumbering giant as he stands up, facing me.

He's brutal. It's not just his height and expansive chest that are intimidating. He has scars up and down his arms, one cutting through his thick, black eyebrow over his left eye. His nose appears to have been broken a few times, but it fits him perfectly. He's rough, wild, and wounded.

I shouldn't know that, but I do. His pain is an entity all its own. It calls to that empty part of me, the part that wonders if I'll always be alone.

My eyes drink in this muscular god of a man, and I have to crane my neck all the way back to take in all of him. He has short black hair and a strong brow. His black eyebrows match his long black lashes, which frame those damn blue eyes. Are they glowing? Why can't I look away? Is he hypnotizing me? Oh god, did he somehow drug me?

"I'm not here to hurt you," he murmurs so softly I hardly hear him. "It's my job to protect you."

I slowly shake my head no, trying to wrap my mind around his words. Why would he protect me?

"The library," he stutters out. "I mean, I'm here to protect the library. I'm the new guard."

Guard. Library. Duh.

"Oh my gosh, of course," I rush to say, smacking my palm on my forehead. "My boss told me you would be starting today. I'm sorry I'm such a spaz," I ramble as I straighten myself up.

"Don't do that," the man grunts. I pause and look up at him, furrowing my brow. "Your head," he says more softly as he points to my forehead. "Don't hit yourself. You could get hurt."

I blink a few times, trying to make sure I heard him right. "Okay..."

"I'm Slater," he blurts out as he grabs my backpack. He hands it to me and our fingers brush, setting my skin ablaze and my heart into overdrive. My knees shake and I suck in a breath, trying to keep myself from suddenly collapsing. "Whoa, I've got you," he whispers, looping an arm around my waist to steady me.

To my complete embarrassment, I press myself against his warm, hard body, burying my face into his chest. I can't stop myself from wrapping my arms around his solid torso and burrowing deeper into his scent, his heat, his strength.

"I've got you," Slater says again, tightening his hold on me.

For one perfect moment, everything is okay.

I'm not being hunted or worrying about bills. I'm not scared. I'm not lonely. My giant is here to protect me.

No, he's here to protect the library.

Right.

I untangle myself from Slater's embrace and take a step back. Cold rushes through me and I shiver from not being close to him anymore.

Slater grunts, which makes me smile. I think he does a lot of that. Why do I find it so endearing?

"Um, okay, well…" I trail off, busying myself with fixing my cardigan and hair. "Welcome. To the library." I grimace at my awkwardness, but Slater isn't laughing or making fun of me. No, the man is stoic, his gaze intently fixed on mine. It makes me feel seen in a way I never knew possible. Like I'm vulnerable yet empowered. Where are these thoughts coming from?

Maybe he really did drug me.

I spin on my heel and walk quickly to the door, needing to get inside and hide somewhere. I fling the door open, intending to run inside and hide in the bathroom, but Slater blocks my entry by stretching his arm across the doorway.

"I already checked the perimeter, but I'll need to go inside first and make sure the place is clear."

Nodding my head, I watch Slater prowl inside with all the grace and brute force of a panther. He favors his right leg, but it's barely perceptible. I only notice because I can't tear my eyes away from him. Questions rapid-fire in my mind, one right after another. I wonder what happened? Is he limping from a recent wound or an old one? Where did his scars come from? Why did it feel so right to be wrapped up in his arms? How can one man rattle me to my core in only a matter of moments?

"All clear," Slater states a few moments later, startling a gasp out of me. He comes into view, motioning me to follow him inside. He tilts his head, eyeing me up curiously. "A little skittish?" he asks.

I snort out a nervous laugh, then clap my hand over my mouth. Slater frowns and circles his fingers around my wrist, gently pulling my hand away.

"No more hitting yourself," he says sternly, looking at my hand as if it personally offends him. I snatch it back and try to compose myself, though I can't help but smile a little bit. Slater is kind of adorable.

"Right. Okay then. Shall I show you the library?"

Slater looks at me, those blue eyes darkening slightly as they dart from my eyes to my lips. "You can show me whatever you want."

My jaw drops at the same time as his. I'm not sure who is more surprised by his words. A second later, Slater clamps his massive hand over his mouth, shaking his head.

"I can't believe I said that," he mutters from behind his hand. Are the tips of his ears red? Oh my god, is he blushing?

"Hey, no hitting yourself, remember?" I say with a little smile.

Slater drops his hand, then runs it through his short hair. Something close to a chuckle leaves his lips. It sounds out of practice, but I'm unreasonably happy that I could make him laugh a bit.

"Okay, give me a tour, *krolik*," he says with more than a little amusement in his deep voice. That sound. God, I swear I feel his voice everywhere, each syllable sinking down into me and making my nerves pop and sizzle.

"*Krolik*?" I ask. Slater lifts one shoulder up in a shrug but doesn't offer an explanation for his pet name. "Right. Um... Follow me," I squeak, dashing ahead of him.

"Anywhere," he murmurs.

Chapter 3

Slater

Magical. Her eyes are magical. Green, gray, and brown flakes sparkle in her gaze, but it's the purple ring around her irises that draws me in.

Though, I'm not looking at her eyes right now.

The short, curvy woman power-walks ahead of me through the library, giving me quite the view. Her wide hips sway back and forth, mesmerizing me with the motion. She thinks she's hiding her juicy curves under her prim and proper slacks and cardigan, but there's no mistaking her round ass and thick thighs.

Fuck, she's got me all messed up. That's why I made a fool of myself in front of her. *You can show me whatever you want.* I mean, what the hell? I don't flirt. I don't play nice. I don't do distractions. I certainly don't do relationships. It wouldn't be fair to unload my baggage and bullshit on someone else.

One look into those hazel eyes, however, has my heart doing silly things like hope for a future. And one look at the rest of her assets has me adjusting my uncomfortably hard dick. I have to get myself under control. The last thing this shy little librarian needs is a battle-scarred monster with a fucking foot-long erection following her around.

"Thanks for coming out here on such short notice," she says over her shoulder as she glides through the hallway into what appears to be a break room. "I'm Raven, by the way."

"I know."

She freezes in her tracks, then turns to face me, wariness creeping into her features. *What are you running from?* I want to ask her. She gave me the same look in the parking lot. God, when she flinched away from me, my chest nearly ripped apart. This precious woman should never be afraid of anything, and definitely not me.

The reasonable explanation is that she's worried about whoever has been creeping around the library. However, the fear in her multi-colored eyes was more than theoretical. She wasn't afraid of the *idea* of someone hurting her. No, my curvy little bunny looked like she saw a ghost of someone who had already done her harm. Even worse, was the thread of certainty and defeat in her purple gaze. Like it was always going to end this way, with someone jumping her in a deserted parking lot.

"I have a roster of library employees and their pictures," I explain, watching Raven's shoulders relax a little at this new information. Her reaction tells me she's been on edge for a while now like she's waiting for someone to uncover some horrible truth about her. My *krolik* needs to feel safe, and that's exactly why I'm here. For the next eight hours, she's under my protection.

And then what? Do you think you can let her go after that?

I shove that thought way down deep, right along with the dangerous feelings threatening to choke me. Jesus, I've been on the job for ten minutes and I'm already going crazy. I need to get my shit together if I'm ever going to survive this assignment.

"Right," Raven says with a nod as she starts to unpack her bag. "Of course. A roster." She mumbles the last few words to herself while taking a travel mug out of her backpack along with a little packet of tea.

I watch in complete fascination as she rinses out her mug and fills it up with hot water from the industrial-sized coffee maker. Her delicate fingers tear open the paper sleeve holding the tea bag, and I have to look away to keep from groaning.

What the hell? How is watching Raven get her morning beverage ready such a turn-on? It makes no sense, but I imagine those soft, porcelain fingers tipped in light pink trailing over my weathered skin and scars. Swallowing thickly, I clear my throat and send the images scattering in my brain.

"Um, would you like some tea?"

I realize I've been staring at her like the starving animal I am. "No," I bark out. I curse myself for not knowing how to act around her. Raven tenses at my harsh tone, but she doesn't jump or gasp, so at least that's an improvement.

"Okay, then," she murmurs to herself.

"I'm sor—"

"Reception is right through here," she cuts me off, twirling ahead of me with her tea in hand. "I'll either be at the front desk or reshelving the new returns. We don't open until ten, and we've been closing by six lately since..." she stops in her tracks, letting her sentence fade away. She nibbles her bottom lip nervously, then clenches and unclenches one of her dainty fists. "Well, since the latest developments," Raven finishes, taking a sip of her drink.

I nod, silently observing her. She doesn't want to talk about the break-in or even label it a break-in. Her travel mug shakes slightly in her hand, and Raven grips it tightly, squeezing the damn thing like it's a life raft. *What aren't you telling me,* krolik?

"I'll stay out of your way," I assure her, hoping to ease some of her anxiety. She snaps her head up and looks in my direction, those calico eyes catching mine. Raven tilts her head to the side, her gaze drifting down my face, neck, and shoulders before meeting my eyes again. Her cheeks turn the lightest shade of pink, and fuck if I don't want to taste her adorable blush.

Adorable.

Who the hell am I right now? More importantly, who is *she*? How did this woman grab a hold of me through a black and white photo, and then knock me on my ass with her beauty in real life?

"You don't have to," she suddenly says. Her eyes go wide and that slight pink on her cheeks turns nearly crimson. "Stay away, I mean. Or, well, of course you have a job. We're not like, hanging out as friends or whatever. I just meant that you... you make me feel safe and I haven't had that in a long time and I... I... never mind."

I'm speechless. She wants me to hang around? I make her feel safe? Wait, she hasn't felt safe in a long time?

"Raven—"

"Okay, I'll just go get started for the day," she rattles out, scurrying around me to get to the reception area.

"Raven," I try again, to no avail.

"If you need anything, I'll be hiding under my desk," she mumbles. I don't think she meant for me to hear that last part. She's flustered and so damn cute as she scurries away from me.

I have to fight the urge to reach out and pull her into my arms. She's so damn skittish, but I know if I held her, I could absorb whatever fears she has. At least for the moment. I'm no one's hero, despite the job description. In the long run, I know my darkness would eat up all of her light. It wouldn't be fair to keep my little bunny as my own. I can protect her this way, though. For now. I can make her feel safe at her place of work.

As much as I want to follow her around, I can tell she needs a little breathing room. Besides, I do have some things to check out from the break-in yesterday. Logan wants me to take notes about the overall security of the library and any suggestions for updates. Colton apparently has a contact who loves revamping older libraries and filling them with books and updated technology, including security cameras.

Sticking to the shadows, I test out old windows and flimsy door locks, taking inventory and texting my findings to Colton. By the time I'm satisfied with reporting all of the weak spots and areas of improvement, the library is open.

Stepping back into the main lobby, I see parents and young children gathered around for storytime in one corner. Several other employees have shown up as well, and everyone is going about their duties quietly and respectfully, much like I would expect from a library.

My eyes skim over the front desk area, hoping for a glimpse of black hair and hazel eyes. I don't see Raven anywhere. I'm sure she's fine. This is no reason to panic.

Taking a few steps closer to reception, I continue to scan the area, not liking this tight feeling in my chest. A tall blonde woman flits around behind a desk, chatting up one of the patrons. An exasperated mother wrangles her two toddlers into one of the aisles with children's books. Still, no sign of Raven.

The front doors swing open, unleashing a wave of unruly high school students here on some field trip or shit. The library fills up with chatter as the teens scout out the space for the best spot. All the talking, rustling of backpacks, and chairs scraping is in direct contrast compared to the peaceful murmurs before the high schoolers got here.

I don't know much about Raven, but I get the sense she'd find this overwhelming. New people, loud noises, blatant disrespect of the rules. I glare at one kid who's sitting on the table with his feet stretched out on a chair. He tilts his chin up, trying to look tough, but when he sees me, his bravado drops. The punk scrambles down and sits in his seat properly.

Raven told me she reshelves new returns when she's not at reception, so I decide to search for her amongst the books. I can still convince myself it's for the job. I need to make sure all of the library employees are safe.

Sure, keep telling yourself that.

As soon as I duck into one of the aisles of books, the loud noises of the main lobby die down to a lull. The shelves block a lot of the sound, making it seem like a private little world back here in the stacks. I can see why my bunny likes it.

Not that she's mine, per se. My responsibility, maybe. My assignment. But not my woman.

A sharp breath escapes my lips and I have to rub the heel of my hand over my chest to ease the sudden ache there. I'm twenty kinds of fucked up. Too fucked up to be in a relationship, and certainly too beastly and raw for a sweet little librarian. Still, the thought of her not being mine has my heart twisting up, seemingly in protest.

A soft sound floats through the air, filtering into my mind and clearing away the chaotic thoughts. I follow as if pulled by a string, hardly aware of my feet carrying me toward the gentle voice.

I turn the corner into another aisle of books, stopping short when I see who the melodic voice belongs to.

Raven is sitting on her knees, humming to herself while organizing a pile of books spread out around her. She looks ethereal, bathed in the mid-morning sun as it streams through the window, little dust motes floating and sparkling all around her.

Her sweet humming stops and her eyes dart to my big boots before slowly sliding up my body. Jesus fuck, I feel her gaze everywhere, gliding up my legs, my torso, and finally, settling on my face.

"Slater," she whispers, her lips parting on a gasp. I refuse to think about her on her knees with her mouth open for an entirely different reason, but Christ...

"Help," I stutter out for some goddamn reason.

Her brows furrow and her hazel eyes twinkle with concern. "You need help?"

"No," I cough out. "You do." I squeeze my eyes shut and rub a hand down my face. I'm terrible at talking to people in general, let alone the most gorgeous, precious, curvy little goddess I've ever seen.

"I do?" she asks, her voice lilting up in what I hope is amusement. I don't like to be made fun of, but I'll be a fool for her if it makes her happy.

When I open my eyes, Raven is looking up at me with a soft yet sassy smile. It's the same one she gave me earlier when she told me not to hit myself. It's the kind of smile I could get addicted to. In fact, I'm pretty sure I already am.

"With the books," I press on for some unknown reason. I just want to be near her, even if I'm a bumbling idiot. When those kaleidoscope eyes are on me, the world doesn't feel like it's caving in. I can breathe. I can just... be.

"You want to help me put books away?" Raven asks. I nod. "Are you sure there isn't something more important for you to do?" I shake my head no. "Will you answer my questions with actual words if I let you stick around?" She quirks an eyebrow up, barely suppressing another addicting smile.

"What do you want to know?" I say with the hint of a chuckle in my voice. It's raspy and unused, but she makes me want to be different. Better. Raven wants my words? I guess I'll have to find some to give her.

Her eyes shine with more green than brown as her smile turns into a grin. Raven hops up and grabs my hands, sending a shockwave through me at the contact. Her softness brushes against my tough, weathered skin, but she doesn't recoil. In fact, I watch in awe as she traces a scar on my palm with the tip of her finger, following the jagged line until it disappears into my sleeve.

Raven gasps softly, her eyes flickering up to meet mine. She looks like she wants to ask me a million questions, but somehow knows I'm not ready to tell her the answers.

With a gentle smile, Raven turns my palms facing up, then steps away briefly to grab a few books. She stacks several books into my hands before picking up a pile of her own. Raven briefly explains the system they have at the library and the corresponding label on each book.

We work for a few moments in silence, Raven putting her stack of books away on one side of the shelf while I put my stack of books away on the other side. I can just see her eyes and eyebrows above the books, and I know she keeps sneaking glances at me while she does her work.

"So... what are your hobbies?" Raven finally asks. I shrug, but she doesn't let me get away with it. "Uh-uh, mister. You said you'd answer with words, remember?"

I roll my eyes, but she knows I'm just teasing. I hope. For all I know, I look deranged.

"I don't have hobbies."

"Psh, everyone has hobbies!" Raven insists. "I bet you work out or run or something. You don't get a body like that from doing nothing." Her eyes nearly pop out of her head and that pink blush creeps up her neck, staining her round cheeks. "I-I... I shouldn't have said that," she mumbles.

I clear my throat to keep from laughing. She's so fucking adorable, and hell yes, I love that she's been checking me out. I never want my bunny to be embarrassed around me, though. So, I tell her something I've never told anyone.

"You're right, I do like to hit the gym. I have another, uh, *hobby* too. It's not really a hobby. I don't know. It's..." I comb my fingers through my hair and rub the back of my neck. "Sometimes I sculpt things," I finally let out after a long exhale. I'm not sure why admitting that makes me feel vulnerable.

I try catching her eyes from between the books, but she's gone. My heart drops to my stomach and I want to kick myself for whatever I said that sent her running. It's for the best. She shouldn't get tangled up in someone like me.

Putting the last book away, I turn to head back out to the main lobby, only I come face to face with the cute little *krolik*.

"You're an artist?" she whispers, her head tilted all the way back so she can meet my gaze. I stare at her hazel eyes, then take in those soft, slightly parted, pink lips. Raven swipes her tongue across her bottom lip, causing my dick to twitch.

"No, no, definitely not. I'm not... I don't do it for... I don't know," I sigh, frustrated at my lack of communication skills. How can I possibly explain that sculpting is the best kind of therapy for my messed up, PTSD brain? She doesn't need to know that. She doesn't need to know any of this.

"I always thought it would be wonderful to create something with my hands," Raven says softly, her eyes never leaving mine. "I just don't have the vision for it, but I admire those who do."

"There's nothing admirable about me, *krolik.*"

"What's that mean? *Krolik*?"

"Bunny," I tell her, loving the way her eyes soften. "It's Russian."

"Oh! Are you from Russia?"

"My mom was a first generation Russian immigrant. She wanted us to keep up the language and traditions of the Motherland." Why the hell did I tell her that?

Raven smiles and nods, absorbing every word. "And why aren't you admirable?" I shrug and look away from her. Raven surprises me yet again by weaving her hand in mine, tugging slightly so I have to bend down closer to her. "You said you'd use your words, remember?"

The knot in my stomach tightens with each breath, sending my heart ricocheting against my rib cage. Fuck, she smells like coconut and vanilla, and I can feel her little breaths against my skin as she continues to tear me apart with her discerning hazel eyes.

What does she want from me? I'm a savage, a killer, a monster. She admires my hands for creating art? What would she think if she knew how many lives these same hands destroyed? How many lives these hands neglected to save?

My skin prickles with awareness, somehow both flushed with heat and freezing cold. Raven brushes her thumb back and forth across my knuckles, silently calming me down.

"I'm no good," I rasp out. "I... I've done things. Fuck," I curse, yanking my hand away from her. I step back, breaking whatever spell she cast over me.

"Slater, it's okay."

"No," I say harshly, hating myself when she flinches away from me. "I'm... I have to check the perimeter."

I tear myself away from the sweetest woman I've ever met, praying she forgets about me and that I haven't scared her too much. Looking over my shoulder, I see Raven staring after me, her lips slightly parted, those damn eyes shining with confusion and hurt. Fuck me, that look cuts deeper than the bomb that destroyed my life.

Fine. I can handle the pain. Raven will forget about me soon enough. Once this assignment is over, I'll be taking a desk job. Clearly, I'm still not ready to be out in public yet.

Chapter 4

Raven

"How long is the hired gun here for?" Missy asks as she fills up her water bottle. "He's scaring away the regulars. Pretty soon it'll be a ghost town in here. Nothing to protect us from except unemployment."

I frown but don't say anything. She's not talking to me anyway. I'd be surprised if Missy even knew I was in the breakroom with her.

Linda snorts out a wicked laugh then gulps down the rest of her coffee. "I wouldn't mind being left alone with him. I bet he's massive *everywhere*." Both women break into giggles and I sink further into my chair, burying my face in my book.

Usually, I can get lost between the pages of the latest thriller or curl up with a steamy romance book and forget the world. Ever since Slater showed up at the library last week, however, I can't seem to concentrate on anything. Whenever I read about a kickass hero, I keep picturing Slater's deep blue eyes, his strong jaw, slight stubble, and furrowed brow. And when my books come to a particularly sexy scene, my mind flashes to what it felt like to be pressed against Slater's chest, the hard slats of his muscles so firm against my soft curves.

I let the fantasy go too far last night. I was so worked up after finishing a book with a growly alpha hero who threw his woman over his shoulder, I slipped my hand between my legs and rubbed myself to images of Slater until I came. Twice.

Yet, I woke up hungry and decidedly more unsatisfied than ever.

It's been seven days of tiptoeing around and sneaking glances at the giant, mysterious bodyguard. It's not enough. We talked that first day, he held me, he opened up, just a little bit. And now? Now, he's ignoring me.

I've replayed our conversation over and over in my mind, trying to figure out where it all went wrong. I called Slater an artist, which he is, and his walls came up so fast I got whiplash. With anyone else, I would have dropped it. I'm not one for confrontation, especially after the last year of my life, but the pain hidden just beneath Slater's harsh words was too much to bear.

The way he talked about himself, how he's not admirable, how he's done bad things… it tore me apart. I hardly know Slater, yet I *know* him. He handled me with such care when he startled me in the parking lot. I can still hear the steady beat of his heart from when I buried my face against his chest. And when I held his hand, surrounded by books and sunlight? I swear Slater trembled as if he could feel the gravity of the moment we were sharing.

But then he ripped his hand away from me and grunted some excuse about checking the perimeter or something. It shouldn't have hurt as much as it did. We shared a moment, so what? At least that's what I keep telling myself every time I catch his deep blue eyes and he looks away or when I start walking toward him and he finds somewhere else to be.

"I'm surprised this one over here didn't pee her pants when he first showed up," Missy whispers loudly to Linda. I know they are talking about me, and as much as I hate it, I don't say anything. What good could come from defending myself? I just need to keep my head down and be thankful for a job and a place to live away from my dad.

Still, my cheeks burn with embarrassment and I hold my book up a little higher, trying to cover up my face.

"Maybe she did," Linda says with a mean laugh, not even trying to be subtle. "She wears the same outfit every day. Maybe she keeps twenty pairs of the same slacks in her backpack." The women snicker, giving me some strong side-eye while I dutifully ignore their comments.

I grew up with money and a closet full of couture dresses, designer purses, and shoes that cost more than my monthly rent now. Even then, I didn't see the big deal. The dresses were uncomfortable and obviously meant to attract attention versus provide coverage and comfort. I don't miss playing dress-up for my father and his business associates.

The clothes I have now are a bit scratchier and stiff, but I get to pick them out. Plus, what's wrong with black slacks? They are perfect for any occasion. Dress them up or down. Or, in my case, dress them with a tank top and a cardigan. I'm a librarian, for goodness sake. This is what we wear!

"Oh, maybe the bodyguard helped her out of her pants!" Missy squeals. "And took that v-card you know she's been carrying around."

I drop my book and stare at the two women in shock. I'm used to them gossipping in front of me, but it's never been this bad before.

"No, she couldn't handle someone like him," Linda says, not missing a beat. "He'd chew her up and spit her out. Besides, the man is a brute. All he does is growl and glare at everyone."

I'm shaking with anger. Slater isn't a brute, he's just quiet.

"Oh shut up. You're just saying that because you tried flirting with him and he didn't take the bait," Missy says with a roll of her eyes. The thought of the tall, gorgeous, blonde-hair, blue-eyed Linda flirting with my Slater has a knot of jealousy forming in my stomach. Not that he's *mine*, but I saw him first. So... finders keepers.

"His loss," Linda snaps. "I bet he's all roided out and can't even get it up. Shame, really. All that muscle and a limp dick to go with it."

"Enough!" I shout, standing up so suddenly my chair scrapes across the floor. Linda and Missy gape at me, and I'll be honest, I think I'm more shocked at my outburst than they are. I can't stop now, though. "You're both petty, shallow people, and you shouldn't be talking about others behind their backs. It's mean and rude and immature."

Missy starts laughing hysterically, but Linda narrows her eyes, piercing me with her hatred. Surprisingly, I don't care. If it were just me they were trash talking, I wouldn't have said anything. But Slater is here to protect us, he's a good man, despite what he seems to think, and he's done nothing to deserve their spiteful words.

"Look who grew a backbone," Linda finally says. Missy laughs again and then changes the subject to her latest Tinder date. Linda keeps her eyes locked on mine for a moment before returning her attention to her friend.

I'm shaking and pulling in ragged breaths as I leave the break room and make a beeline straight for the bathroom. After taking a few calming breaths and washing my face with cold water, I feel a little more in control.

I can't explain what happened back there. Usually, their insults roll off my back. Some hurt worse than others, but I've mostly resigned to the fact that they're miserable people who want to make others miserable as well.

But I couldn't just let them throw Slater under the bus. Okay, fine, maybe some of my anger came from the sharp sting of jealousy when I thought about Slater and Linda together, but mostly I just wanted them to shut up.

Stepping out into the hallway, I decide to visit the section on arts and crafts. We don't get a lot of DIYers at this library, probably because the selection is a bit lacking, but it's my job to make sure each section is organized and easily accessible. And if I happen to find a book on clay sculpting that I could recommend to Slater, that would just be a bonus.

Not that he'd let me get close enough to hand it to him.

I know I should leave him alone, but I can't. My body is tuned to his, and I swear I can feel his presence long before I ever see him. Whenever the tall, silent bodyguard is within eyesight, I gravitate toward him, even though I know he won't let me get close enough to talk let alone touch.

But God, I crave his touch. It's getting worse and worse each day. And after last night's little session starring Slater, the empty ache between my thighs is almost unbearable.

I tuck a few loose strands of hair back into the bun at the base of my neck, then smooth out my cardigan. No sense getting hot and bothered in the middle of the workday.

Making my way over the arts and crafts section, I pick up a few stray books and reshelve them, straightening up things here and there and making the space look nice and clean.

Something catches my eye and I turn to look out the closest window. The bushes outside rustle and then a dark figure emerges, peering inside. I drop the books I'm holding, ice filling my veins. I can't make out any details about the person lurking in the shadows, but I know who it is.

The same person I've been running from for months. The same person who I suspect broke in last week. My father sent his muscle, Paul, after me, and it looks like the man is getting closer and closer to his target.

I didn't want to believe the suspicious activity was my past trying to claw its way into my present. I feel terrible for bringing my drama to work and potentially putting others in danger. I'll have to apologize later, however.

Clenching my fists at my sides, I take a few steps backward. I need to get away from the window, away from the prying gaze of the man who wants to kidnap me and force me back into the life I escaped from.

My breath is lodged somewhere in my throat, and my stomach turns in on itself, threatening to spill my lunch all over the floor. I'm shaking from head to toe, every muscle tense as I take another step back. The man is still mostly hidden in the shadow of the building and the bushes, but I know he's there. I know he's looking. Planning. Calculating.

Someone grabs my shoulder from behind and I scream, spinning around and backing away as quickly as I can. My feet get tangled together and I start to fall backward, but then I'm surrounded by warmth and solid arms wrapping around me, holding me close.

Slater.

Fear, longing, loneliness, and exhaustion all crash into me at once, pulling a sob from somewhere deep in my soul. Tears pour down my face as I bury it against Slater's chest. I cling to him like he's the only thing keeping me grounded, and truthfully, he is. I might dissolve into a pile of tears and trauma if he weren't here holding me up.

"You're safe, *krolik*," he murmurs. The deep rumble of his voice pours over me, covering me in a shield of protection. I'm completely consumed by his strength, his wintergreen scent, his steady breath, and his calming heartbeat.

"S-s-sorry," I stutter out, sniffling as I peel myself off of his chest. Coldness sweeps through me at the loss of contact, and I shiver. Slater is still holding my hips, and he tightens his grip on me like he doesn't want to let me go.

"What happened?" he asks, pulling me closer so I'm pressed up against him again. I give in to his touch, closing my eyes as I rest my cheek against his chest once more, right over his heart.

I can't remember the last time someone just held me, aside from Slater in the parking lot a week ago. The staff at home raised me as well as they could, and the tutors I grew up with gave me a great education, but there wasn't a whole lot of love or cuddles. Everything was formal, as if we were about to enter an important business meeting at the drop of a hat.

But being cradled right here in Slater's arms is everything I've been missing in my life. He strokes a hand up and down my spine while cupping the back of my neck, massaging the tension out of my muscles.

"I s-saw s-someone," I finally admit. "In the window. Hiding in the bushes." Slater growls and every muscle in his body flexes. I can feel the animal in him rising up, ready to tear apart any and every threat.

Before I realize what's happening, Slater untangles from me and shoves me behind him, keeping a hand on my hip while reaching for his gun with the other. I fist his shirt and nuzzle into his back, completely hidden by his broad, muscular frame.

"He's gone now," I whisper. Slater grunts. Despite the circumstances, I smile at his response.

"I still need to go check it out."

"Don't leave me," I whimper out miserably. I'm pathetic and needy, and I know Slater doesn't want to deal with my mess of emotions right now. "Never mind," I say quickly, taking a step back from him.

Slater turns toward me, those dark blue eyes finding mine. He pins me in place with one look, then shocks me by cupping my chin. His touch is overwhelmingly gentle like I'm precious and he doesn't want to break me.

For a long moment, we just stare at each other. I don't know what's going on in his head, but I see some battle going on just beneath the surface. His eyes hold such tension and concern. I also see confusion, like I'm some great mystery to him.

"I'll be right back, *krolik*. I'm not leaving you."

"But—"

"Let's get you to the break room where you can gather your things." Slater's voice is steady and certain as he guides me back out to the main lobby with a hand at the small of my back. I keep my head down, not wanting anyone to see my tear-stained face.

Slater senses my insecurity and wraps his arm around my waist, tucking me into his side as we make our way to the break room.

"Gather your things, Raven. I'll check outside and then talk to your boss. You've had a scare and I'm taking you home."

"No, it's really okay, I'm just... I'm just frazzled. Maybe it was nothing. I'm just seeing things." I hate that this is affecting my job. I already feel guilty enough that they're spending money on a bodyguard because of my mess.

"Do you trust me?"

"Slater, it's not that I—"

"Do you trust me?"

"I'm just—"

"Do you trust me?" Those blue eyes plead with me to take a leap, to give him my trust.

I finally nod, surrendering to his care. It's not just my trust I handed over. I'm pretty sure this man already has my heart.

"Good girl," he whispers, surprising me yet again when he leans down and presses his lips to my forehead. I close my eyes as he breathes me in, savoring the feeling of being this close. "Stay here," he instructs before walking out and leaving me alone with my thoughts.

I have no idea what's going to happen next, but I'm confident that Slater will be by my side.

Chapter 5

After talking to the manager and putting in a call to the Watchdog office to get someone to take my place at the library, I loaded Raven into my SUV. She's still pale and shaking as she gives me directions to her apartment, but at least I know she's safe.

Jesus Christ, I'm still not exactly sure what happened, but I fucking felt her fear from the shadows where I was observing her.

Yes, I've kept an eye on my bunny this last week, even if she doesn't know it. I can't seem to help it. I needed to know she's safe and happy at all times, though I couldn't bring myself to talk to her again.

She got under my skin that first day. Fuck that, she tore me open and burrowed straight into my soul, setting it on fire. It was too much. She was trying to infuse her goodness and light into me with those damn magical eyes, but I couldn't allow it. I carry around an endless black void inside my chest, and I knew I'd suck up any kindness she showed me.

I was doing another check around the lobby when I caught sight of Raven stepping out of the bathroom. She looked rattled, and I wondered if it was something Martha and Lydia said in the break room. Or is it Maya and Lauren? Mary and Lucy? I've never been very good at names.

I followed my little bunny into a smaller, quieter part of the library and watched her fuss over book placement and cluttered tables. Everything about her is mesmerizing. I took my attention away from her for thirty seconds to check my phone, and that's all it took.

Something scared the shit out of her, and I will never forgive myself for not getting to her sooner. I was only twenty feet away, but if I had been watching her more closely, maybe she wouldn't have gotten spooked. I'm failing her already, but I have no choice but to keep her close. I won't risk her sense of safety again.

"It's that building," she whispers, pointing to an old apartment complex in desperate need of a facelift.

I nod and turn into the parking lot. Raven takes a deep breath and exhales it forcefully as if trying to shake off whatever sent her into a panic attack. It makes sense that she'd be rattled at seeing a shadowy figure outside with all the weirdness going on and the break-in, but her reaction was over the top.

The fear ran deeper than a potential burglar or even a stalker. When I held her in my arms, she clung to me and let her emotions roll through her, unleashing what felt like years of sadness and pain. It damn near broke me to see her like that, but I had to be strong for her. I still do. I'll get to the bottom of what's really going on and make sure Raven has nothing to fear.

I park the SUV in front of her building and hop out, running around to her side of the vehicle. Opening the door, I lean down and unbuckle Raven's seatbelt before kissing her forehead. She softens at my touch, making me feel like the king of the world. I don't know what it is about her, but I long to have her in my arms, my lips pressed against hers, our bare skin touching every-fucking-where.

Raven steps out of the car and I scoop her up, grunting in satisfaction when she curls into my embrace. She produces a set of keys for me, and I frown, not liking that she's living alone on the bottom floor of a place that has sketchy security at best. I'll have to fix that, but for now, my *krolik* needs rest.

Inside, her apartment is tinier than I expected. Then again, almost every room feels small when you're as huge as I am. I take up damn near half the space and have to duck my head to get in through the doorway.

I carry her to the couch, which is nothing more than a loveseat that looks as run down as the building itself. Not that I'm judging her at all. I can tell Raven has tried making the place homey and comfortable, but it still tugs at my heart that she's been living in a dump. I have so many questions for her, but I don't want to overwhelm my little bunny.

Carefully sitting down, I keep Raven in my arms and get her situated on my lap. I take up the entire couch, so there's nowhere else for her to sit. And even if there was, I'd want her right here.

"Can you tell me what happened?" I ask softly. Or, as softly as someone like me can manage.

"I just saw someone. That's all. It was probably nothing."

I tip her chin up with one finger, forcing her to meet my gaze. "We both know that's not true, *krolik*. How can I protect you if I don't know what the threat is? Did you recognize the person outside the window?"

Raven looks down at her lap, wringing her hands together nervously. I place one hand over both of hers, hoping to calm her down.

"I thought your job was to protect the library." I can tell she's trying to be sassy with me, but her voice is hollow.

"And now my job is to protect you." Raven looks up at me, tears shimmering in her eyes as she debates whether to tell me her secrets. "You said you trusted me earlier," I remind her. "So trust me with this."

She hesitates for a moment before nodding her head and then resting it on my shoulder. I wrap an arm around her waist, keeping her close while she breaks her heart open for me.

"I grew up in New York City," she begins, pausing briefly before continuing. "After my mom left when I was ten, it was just my dad and me. He didn't really know what to do with me. I think I reminded him of my mom. My dad threw himself into his career, opening a hedge fund and growing his millions. He was always kind of... cold, I guess. I was used to him ignoring me, so I was surprised when he threw me a big party when I turned eighteen."

"How old are you?" I blurt out. God, I knew she was young, but...

"Twenty."

I nod, kissing the top of her head. I can't help it. She's sixteen goddamn years younger than me, but that only makes my possessive, protective instinct stronger.

"What happened at the party?"

She sighs and snuggles against me. My woman has been deprived of love and attention for most of her life, and she seems to be soaking up every touch. I guess I'll just have to hold her more often. I don't know anything about caring for someone as precious as Raven, but I'll figure it out. I have to protect and cherish her. I feel it taking over every muscle, every bone, every cell in my body.

"Nothing, really," she continues. "And yet everything. It all changed. I could tell instantly I was being shown off. I didn't have many friends growing up, but the few I kept weren't even there. Instead, my dad invited a bunch of his investors and business contacts. He had me wear this awful red dress that practically cut off my circulation, it was so tight!"

Raven rolls her eyes, but I don't join her little laughter. The thought of her body on display for hungry, horny assholes has me thinking murderous thoughts. "Jesus, Raven, did anyone touch you?" I growl.

"No, nothing like that. But the birthday party was just the beginning. Every weekend, my dad dressed me up and took me out to parties. In the back of my head, I knew he was using me to lure in business contacts. I couldn't quite make myself believe it though. But then he set me up on a date with some old guy."

"Fucking dead man," I snarl under my breath.

Raven looks up at me, a little grin pulling at her lips. It soothes my raw, bleeding heart to see her eyes shining with something other than tears. She cups the side of my face and I lean into her touch. I don't think anyone has ever handled me so gently before.

She drops her hand and settles back down, nestling her head between my neck and shoulder. "Anyway, my dad refused to let me back out of the date. He kept setting me up with these terrible men, though thankfully no one took advantage of me." I grunt and nod my head, thankful for that much at least. "Then last year, my dad threw a huge party to celebrate some big new business venture. I had no idea the deal came with so many strings attached."

"What do you mean?"

"The party doubled as an engagement announcement... *my* engagement announcement to his new business partner."

"What the fuck?!" I roar. Raven flinches and I immediately soften, wrapping her up in my arms. "Sorry, *krolik*. I just... goddamnit."

Raven nods and sighs. I can feel the energy draining out of her, but I need to know the rest.

"After the party, my dad and I got in a huge fight. I've never seen him so angry. His eyes were black and his face contorted as he yelled at me to shut up and play my part. He said... he said the only reason he kept me around was because he knew I'd be useful one day."

"Jesus," I grunt, barely holding back the long list of other expletives I'd like to shout out.

"I was planning on leaving, but he somehow figured it out. My dad locked me in my room for a week, allowing me two bathroom breaks and two meals a day."

Some tortured, feral sound rumbles up from the pit of my stomach. "He locked you in your room?" I snarl. I can think of at least twenty different ways to kill this motherfucker, but that's not what Raven needs right now.

I tap into a reservoir of strength I didn't know I had and pull back the murderous rage. With a deep, cleansing breath, I press my lips to Raven's forehead, encouraging her to continue.

"He thought he broke me," she whispers. "I went along with his plan and earned his trust back little by little until he allowed me to go to a gala with my husband-to-be. I didn't have time to think, I just knew I'd never get another opportunity. So, I ran. I've been here in Chicago for six months, and I thought maybe he'd given up the search, but then..."

"Then he sent someone after you and they broke into the library," I finish for her, fury boiling in my veins. "Why didn't you go to the police?"

"I didn't know for sure. Plus, my dad has so many connections and I was scared he already got some of the cops on his side. He's been known to pay off police and other officials. I know it was stupid and selfish of me to put everyone at the library in danger, but I didn't know what to do. I didn't know..."

"Shh, baby girl," I whisper, kissing her forehead. That small gesture makes her melt every single time. I make a note to do it more often. "I wasn't accusing you of anything. I just want to know what we're up against."

"We?"

God, her voice is so small, so tentative, so full of hope. "Yes, Raven. I'm right here, and I won't let anything happen to you. Do you trust me?"

"You know I do," she murmurs. "I just don't understand why you want to help. Why me?"

"Why you?" I ask incredulously. "Raven, you're... you're... shit, I'm not good with words, but I'm trying to be for you. I can't explain this pull, this connection, but you've wrecked me, little *krolik*. Knocked me on my ass with one look. I tried to keep my distance because I didn't want to hurt you, but I can't stay away anymore."

"Then don't," she whispers, tipping her chin up to meet my gaze. "The only way you can hurt me is by leaving. Please don't leave."

I fucking can't take it anymore.

I close the distance between us, getting my first taste of Raven's sweet lips.

She threads her fingers in my hair and pulls me closer, a soft moan falling from her lips. I instantly melt for her, sinking into her sweetness and letting my hands map out her curves. Raven wiggles against me and I growl into her mouth as I lift her up, readjusting her so she's straddling me.

Oh fuck.

I can feel the heat of her pussy through our clothes as she grinds down on me. I know my woman is inexperienced, but her body knows what to do.

Slipping my hands underneath her chaste little sweater has me feeling like a goddamn beast ravaging a sweet little princess. It makes me a filthy fucker, but I love it. My cock throbs at the thought of ripping her demure outfit off and pounding her tight cunt until we both come undone.

Not yet. It's too much too soon, but I can still give my girl what she so desperately needs.

I trail my fingers up her back, loving the way her bare skin heats under my touch. When I slide my hands around to her front, Raven sucks her stomach in as if I'd somehow be disappointed. Breaking our kiss, I cover her rounded stomach with both hands and rest my forehead against hers.

"Every part of you is beautiful, baby girl," I murmur. She nibbles on her bottom lip, her eyes shining more blue than green right now. Raven doesn't quite believe me, so I decide to show her how goddamn sexy she is.

I slowly unclasp the button on her pants, then tug down the zipper. She inhales sharply, and I swallow down the sound with a kiss.

"Is this okay?" I rasp against her lips, sliding a hand into her pants and cupping her pussy. Fuck, her panties are *soaked*, her cream covering my fingers as I grind them against her center.

"Oh my God," Raven moans. "Please, please, please... It's never felt this good."

I growl and start kissing a line down her neck and then back up to her mouth where I pull her bottom lip between my teeth. I swallow her moan before diving back in for another kiss.

I should slow down, let her catch her breath and rest after the day she's had, but all bets are off once she starts grinding down on my hand. My fingers find their way inside her damp panties, and I stroke her slit up and down, gathering up her juices. Cupping her ass with my free hand, I help her find her rhythm as I continue drowning in her kiss.

When I rub her swollen little clit, Raven moans and jerks, throwing her head back. I attach my lips to her now exposed neck, nipping and kissing down the slender column.

I want her so bad it hurts, but I know it won't be today. She's been through too much. I can give her what she wants though. What she needs. I circle her pulsing entrance with one blunt finger before nudging just the tip inside.

"Oh my God!" she moans.

"You like that, *krolik*? Like when I touch you? When I play with your pussy?"

"Yes, Slater..."

I pinch her little bundle of nerves and am rewarded with another moan. I kiss my way down to her perky breasts, looking up at her and silently asking permission. Raven smiles wickedly as she unbuttons her sweater and tosses it behind her. I'm struck dumb at the sight of her in a tight little tank top, her breasts stretching the fabric and showing off her pebbled nibbles.

Unable to hold myself back any longer, I lean forward and cover one with my mouth, through the fabric of her thin tank top. Another cry of ecstasy falls from her lips.

Sinking one finger further into her throbbing channel, I nearly come from how tight and wet she is. Raven's whole body trembles as she lets out a shaky whimper. She feels fucking incredible. Her silk walls pulse around my finger as I curl it up to find her G-spot. At the same time, my thumb presses and rubs her clit.

"Oh, fu... Oh, God... Don't stop!"

I love her breathless cries, letting me know how lost she is in this. In *us*. I suck on her left nipple through the shirt, pumping my finger in and out of her while applying steady pressure to her clit. I can tell all of the sensations are overwhelming her curvy body as she shakes all around me. I curl my finger and press on her clit while biting down on her nipple and she fucking explodes in my hands.

Raven whimpers my name and throws her head back, squeezing her eyes shut, while her pussy clamps down on my finger again and again. I feel her juices pooling in my hand as her orgasm devastates her. It's the sexiest thing I've ever seen, knowing I put that look of pleasure on my woman's face, knowing I worked her body till she fell apart. I fucking come in my pants while she writhes on top of me, riding out her pleasure.

My little bunny collapses in my arms, resting her sweaty forehead on my shoulder.

"Oh my *God*, Slater. That was... I've never felt so good."

I choke out a groan as my dick jerks and releases one more wave of cum. Jesus fucking Christ.

"Are you alright?" I ask after a few moments of silence. Raven lets out a huge breath and nods, leaning up slightly to look me in the eye. Her normally perfect bun is askew, sending black strands of hair flowing around her face and over her shoulders. Her lips are swollen, her cheeks bright pink, and she looks so completely adorable and disheveled it makes my heart ache.

"Yeah, you can do that anytime," she replies with a sleepy little grin. Fuck, she's cute.

I kiss the tip of her nose, then lift her up in my arms, carrying her about ten feet until we reach the bed. I silently strip off her pants, groaning when I see her white panties. However, it's not about that. Not right now, at least.

Pulling the blanket over my little bunny, I make sure to tuck her in tight before leaning down to kiss her forehead. Just like every other time, Raven softens, giving me a sweet smile when I stand up.

"Rest now, *krolik*. I have some business to take care of, but I'll always protect you. You're safe."

Raven looks like she's about to protest, but she's cut off by a yawn. I smirk at her and then wink, shocking both of us. It's worth it to see her blush. Giving her one last kiss, I head out the door and hop into my SUV.

Circling the block a few times, I park across the street from her apartment building, under a tree that will provide some good coverage. Once I'm satisfied that I have a good view of Raven's front door, I pull out my phone and call Logan, giving him an update. We both agree to still keep someone stationed at the library, but our priority, *my* priority is Raven.

After hanging up, I settle in for a long night of watching over my woman. It's been a long damn time since I've had a purpose, and never one as important as this. No harm will come to my *krolik*. Not while I'm here.

Chapter 6

Raven

I was a little disappointed that Slater didn't stay with me last night, but it was probably for the best. My emotions were all over the place, and honestly, I was so drained, I fell asleep minutes after he left.

Still, a part of me hoped I'd wake up in his arms this morning. I should just be thankful I got any rest at all. After having a breakdown at the library and then spilling my heart out to Slater, I didn't think I'd be able to calm down enough to sleep.

Then again, that orgasm he gave me was enough to clear my mind and zap my energy. I mean... holy hell, I didn't know *anything* could feel that good. I think I finally understand why people love sex so much.

I fan my face, trying to cool down the heat rushing through me at the memory. "Get it together," I hiss at myself in the bathroom mirror.

After I finish getting ready for the day, I check my cupboards and make a shopping list. It's my day off, and like it or not, I have errands to run. I get that familiar sinking, twisting feeling in my stomach at the thought of going out.

The first few months I was in Chicago, I had a panic attack almost every time I stepped out of my apartment. I'm vulnerable out on the streets. The anxiety never left me, but the overwhelming, suffocating panic subsided as time went on.

I'm right back into fight or flight mode now. My hand shakes as I reach for the doorknob, my breath coming out in shallow pants. What if he's right outside the door, waiting to grab me?

If he knew where you lived, he would have come for you last night, I remind myself.

A shiver runs down my spine and cold sweat beads on my upper lip. I'm both thankful that the man my father sent doesn't seem to have figured out where I live and terrified at the reality of how much danger I'm in.

As I turn the door handle, I brace myself for the open parking lot and sunlight beating down from the clear summer sky. There's nowhere for me to hide out there. I don't even have a car, I just walk everywhere.

I notice, not for the first time, how flimsy the door is. Hell, someone could easily unscrew the handle or the hinges and let themself right in. I bet they wouldn't even need to bother with removing hardware. The door is ancient and run down like the rest of this dump. A good kick would probably splinter the wood.

Maybe it's safer outside after all.

Taking a deep breath, I steady my heartbeat before cracking open the door and peeking outside. I don't see anyone, so I inch the door open a little more, enough to stick my head out. I still don't see anyone, so I step outside and lock the door, though I don't think it would do much to keep anyone out.

When my eyes have adjusted to the bright sun, I notice a familiar vehicle parked right across the street. My feet carry me over there before my brain has a chance to catch up. The tinted driver's side window slowly rolls down, and for a second, I wonder if I made a mistake. I have no idea who is in this SUV, only that it looks like Slater's.

I stop a few feet away, then let out a forceful sigh of relief to see the top of Slater's short black hair. As the window moves down, revealing more of his features, I can't stop from squeezing my thighs together.

I love every brutal inch of this man. The scar that runs through his thick black eyebrow, those intense blue eyes, his lips, which are surprisingly soft yet commanding. He exudes the kind of power and strength most men dream of without even trying.

"Morning, bunny," Slater says, the corner of his mouth pulling up into a hint of a smile. God, I want to see his real smile, the one I know he hasn't shown anyone in a long time. I don't know if I'd survive that much beauty and masculinity all at once, but what a way to go.

"Hi," I squeak out, sounding like a schoolgirl with a silly crush. "What are you doing here?"

"I said I'd always protect you," he replies with a shrug. It takes me a beat to figure out what he means.

"You stayed out here all night?" Slater nods. "What... why?" My eyes are wide and my mouth is nearly hanging open. He really sat in his car and kept watch while I slept? It's too much.

Tears burn the back of my eyes, but I blink them away, hoping to hide them from the man who is quickly undoing everything I've ever known about men. Slater is too perceptive, though.

He slides out of the SUV and closes the distance between us, cupping my face in his hands. Slater leans forward and kisses my forehead, resting his lips there and breathing me in.

"Because you're mine," he murmurs.

"Y-yours?"

"That's right. It's my job to protect you."

"Oh. Right." I try not to let the disappointment show as I dip my head down, breaking the connection between us. Of course, Slater sees right through me.

"Wait, no, not my job," he quickly follows up, running a hand through his hair. "At least, not the one I was hired for. I... shit, I can't explain it, Raven. I... you give me purpose. It's my *honor* to protect you. I'm not good with words, but—"

I fling myself into his arms, cutting him off with a kiss. "I like your words," I whisper onto his lips before kissing him again. Slater groans and angles me so he can taste more, kiss me deeper, and drive me completely crazy.

We're both breathless by the time we break apart. Slater surprises me by engulfing me in a hug. I'm completely surrounded by his wintergreen scent, his firm muscles, and the undeniable strength coursing through him with each breath.

"Thank you," I whisper into his chest. I'm not sure he heard me, but then Slater gives me one last squeeze and tips my chin up.

"No, *krolik*. Never thank me. You've given me my life back, baby girl."

I don't understand what he means, but the raw emotion in his deep blue gaze is overwhelming. I want to know everything about him. How did he get his scars? What kinds of things does he sculpt? What motivates him? Does he like his coffee black or with a bit of creamer? I can already tell he doesn't have his coffee with sugar.

"Let me take you out to coffee," I blurt out. I don't really have the extra funds for two coffees, but I'll figure that out later. For now, I can at least learn this one thing about him. Maybe he'll finally be comfortable enough to show me more of his secrets.

"Coffee?" Slater questions, as if it's a completely foreign concept to him.

"To thank you for staying out here all night."

"What did I say about thanking me?" he asks, leaning in to brush his lips against the shell of my ear.

"Well, what if I want to get to know you?" I hold my breath as he processes what I just said. Did I really ask the most devastatingly rugged and handsome man I've ever seen out on a coffee date? I can hardly believe it myself.

Slater gives me another fragment of a smile. I feel the warmth all the way through my body, settling somewhere deep in my bones. "I'll agree to coffee, little bunny, but only if I can make it for us in my home." He must sense my shock, because he adds, "I'm not very good with, uh, people. I'm not really... fit to be in public."

"What? Why do you think that?" I reel back, placing my hand over my heart. It physically pains me to think Slater has been isolating himself because he somehow feels unworthy.

"Let me take you to my place and maybe I'll tell you," he quips, motioning me toward his SUV.

I smile and let him lead me to the passenger's side with a hand at the small of my back. "Did you just flirt with me, Slater?" I tease as he opens the door for me.

"If you have to ask, I must not be doing it right," he grumbles. His tone is grumpy, but the sparkle in his crystal blue eyes shows a more playful side to him I haven't seen before.

I give him a big smile, then giggle when he presses kisses all over my face. How can Slater be unbearably rugged and sexy while also being adorable and cuddly? I have no idea, but I want to keep him as mine. He said I'm his, so it makes sense that the giant teddy bear bodyguard belongs to me, too.

We drive in comfortable silence to Slater's house. His hand slips into mine after a few minutes, and he squeezes as if proving to himself I'm still here.

I'm not surprised when Slater pulls into a cabin on the outskirts of the city. I couldn't imagine him living in the hustle and bustle of Chicago. A man like Slater needs space, and not just because he's so freaking huge.

He helps me out of the SUV, tucking me into his side as we walk up to his front door. I nestle against him, savoring every touch, every point of contact. I didn't realize how starved I was for human connection on that level until Slater held me and fused his lips and soul with mine.

Slater lets us inside and I pause to look around. The place is minimal and mostly empty, void of any personal touches. A large black couch sits along one wall, and a pristine bookshelf is right next to it. I find myself walking toward the books, grinning when I realize they are organized by genre and then the author's last name.

"I redid it after that first day at the library," Slater says, stepping up behind me. He loops his arms around my waist and presses me against his hard chest. "I think of you every time I look at it."

I gasp and then moan softly when he nips at my neck then kisses away the sting. "Slater..." I whimper, the desperate sound making him tighten his hold on me.

"Yeah, baby girl?" he rasps.

Slater doesn't give me a chance to answer. He spins me around and presses me against the nearest wall, crashing his lips down on mine. His tongue thrusts inside my mouth, stroking me and claiming me, and making me soak my panties.

"Oh, God," I moan, tearing my mouth away from his. I suck down air as Slater smoothes his hands up and down my body, pausing to squeeze and rub my curves appreciatively.

"Gotta stop, Raven" he grunts into the side of my neck before licking me there and catching the tender skin between his teeth. "I can't hold back much longer, and I don't want to scare you away."

"I'm not scared," I breathe out. "I can't hold back either. I just... I don't know what I'm doing. Can you show me?"

"Fuck," he growls, attacking my lips as he presses his body further into mine, pinning me against the wall. "Are you wet for me, Raven? Is my dirty girl wet for me?"

I let out a throaty moan and nod. "Will you... Can you... T-touch me there?"

"Fuck yes," he grits out, cupping my pussy and rubbing my aching center over my pants. "Goddamn, I feel your heat. Do you need something from me? Need me to make you come again?"

His words are so filthy, but they trigger something inside of me. This man has reduced me to base urges I didn't think I had until I met him. I nod and roll my hips, trying to get him to somehow touch me deeper, more, more, more...

Slater nips at my chin, my pulse point, my shoulder, and then slips his hand into my slacks. I know he feels how soaked I am, and it only turns him on more.

"Jesus," he grunts, stroking my pussy and parting my folds over my panties. The fabric scrapes against my sensitive clit, making me shiver and moan.

"More," I beg, gripping his meaty biceps and digging my nails in.

Slater plays with the waistband of my panties, teasing me and driving me absolutely wild. Finally, *finally*, he touches me where I'm throbbing for him, swiping two fingers up my slit and circling my clit.

"Raven, shit, baby, this cunt is so fucking juicy," he grunts. My pussy contracts at his dirty words, trying to suck him inside. He groans and continues to stroke me up and down, gathering my arousal and massaging my little ball of nerves.

I squeeze my eyes shut and moan, throwing my head back and exposing my neck to his greedy mouth. Slater sucks on the side of my neck and dips one finger into my tight hole, making me grind down on his hand. "Oh," I gasp, pulsing around him and releasing even more wetness.

"So fucking tight. You're gonna feel fucking incredible wrapped around my dick, aren't you, *krolik*? Do you want me to stretch out this little cunt of yours?"

"Mmm..." I nod frantically, shifting my hips and forcing his finger deeper inside of me. "Fuck!" I cry out.

Suddenly, Slater removes his hand, leaving me empty and confused. I open my eyes and see Slater kneeling in front of me, gliding his hands up and down my thighs. "I need to taste you. Just one taste. Is that okay? Can I make you come on my tongue?"

"God yes," I whimper. I don't even care that I'm begging him. Slater created this mess, now he needs to lick it up. Who am I right now? Whose filthy thoughts are these? I don't have time to think about that for long. Slater practically rips my pants open, tugging them down my legs along with my soaking panties.

"Jesus, how do you smell so good?" he says more to himself than to me.

Slater slips my shoes off and helps me step out of my pants, staring at my pussy the whole time. I tremble as he ghosts his fingers up my legs, guiding one over his shoulder, exposing me completely to him.

"Perfect, just like the rest of you," he whispers right before parting my lips with his tongue and sucking on my clit. Hard.

I buck my hips and grab his hair, overwhelmed by the sensation of his warm tongue against my sensitive, swollen clit. He growls into my pussy, the vibrations rattling my bones as he devours me.

Slater spears his tongue into my entrance and swirls his nose around my clit. My breaths come out as short little gasps as my muscles tense and pulse. It's unlike anything I've ever experienced. I feel myself teetering on the edge, close, so close to falling over into the unknown.

A strangled scream comes out instead as I explode on his tongue. I jerk in his arms, but Slater grips me tighter, steadying my movements even as he laps at me and bats my clit around, prolonging my pleasure.

He looks up at me right as I tip my head down to look at him. His eyes are stormy, dark, and feral. I see my juices covering his lips and nose, making me moan. Slater doesn't give me any time to recover before flattening his tongue and licking me from bottom to top.

"Oh, ohmygod, Slater, I... I can't..."

He grunts and continues to nibble and suck on my folds. The world crashes down around me until all I can focus on are the relentless strokes of his tongue as he pushes me higher and higher, winds me tighter and tighter, increasing the pressure in my core almost unbearably.

I gasp and writhe as he plunges two fingers inside of me and curls them up, hitting some spot inside me that makes my nerves light up and burn deliciously beneath my skin. He swirls his tongue around my clit again and again. I can't breathe. My heart thrashes. There's a rushing sensation flooding my body. I feel like I have to twist away, back down from the onslaught of pleasure, but I can't. I'm rooted in place, completely at his mercy.

My whole body gets tight. The pressure builds inside me, through my pelvis, over my skin, in my muscles, and along nerves. Pleasure swells and explodes as I convulse in his arms. He pins me to the wall, mercilessly eating me out with a growl. My sweaty flesh shakes as I jerk and fight my way through my orgasm.

"Oh baby," he raises his face to stare at me in awe. "You squirted all over me. Shit, you're incredible. Love making this perfect little pussy gush."

I'm floating through space, through bliss, through lust and release. There's a rhythmic, sharp throbbing between my legs that brings me down from my high. I open my eyes and see Slater slowly licking me up and down, swallowing down all of me, every last drop.

My bones turn to liquid as I slump against the wall completely wrung out. Slater helps me get dressed and then stands up, pulling me into his chest. He holds me up and kisses me, letting me taste myself. He groans and I bury my face in his chest, not sure what happens next.

"Are you okay, bunny? You're shaking," he whispers. "Was that too much?"

"It was perfect," I mumble from where my face is pressed against his firm muscles. Slater chuckles, the warm, rich sound filling me up and making me smile along with him.

"Yeah, it was. *You* were." He kisses the tip of my nose and then steps away, chuckling again when I pout. "I promised you coffee, didn't I?"

"I'm okay with the change of plans."

Slater rewards me with another smile, then he weaves his fingers in mine and tugs me along. "My girl can have orgasms *and* coffee. No need to choose one over the other."

I giggle and follow him, repeating his words in my head. *My girl.* I want to be his in every way.

Chapter 7

Slater

The oven beeps at the same time as the microwave. I spin around in my kitchen, opening the microwave and then slamming it shut again before hitting the timer on the oven.

What the hell was I thinking inviting Raven over for dinner? As if I know how to cook anything decent. I just want to be with her, be around her, smell her sweetness, and feel her curvy little body pressed against mine.

We couldn't very well cook in her apartment. From what I saw, my girl's kitchen consists of a hotplate and a mini-fridge. I'll be moving her in with me as soon as she agrees to it. In the meantime, I want to get to know everything about her.

Since going out to a restaurant isn't an option, not only for her safety but for my sanity, we decided to have dinner at my place. Brilliant. Except I have no idea what the fuck I'm doing.

I have seasoned chicken cooking on the stovetop and potatoes in the oven. I thought we might need some sort of vegetable, so I grabbed a can of corn and warmed it up in the microwave. It's not much, but I can learn. I'll make Raven the most mouthwatering dinner she's ever had if she sticks with me.

I'm so far gone for this girl already. Every damn time those magical multi-colored eyes land on me, a possessive wave of lust washes over me. It's more than that, though. The possessiveness is only amplified by how fucking sweet and adorable she is.

I let out a dry laugh and shake my head as I check on the potatoes. Adorable? Colton would give me so much shit if he knew I was even thinking that word, let alone attributing it to a woman. It's true though. Raven is the whole goddamn package. It only becomes clearer the more time we spend together. The more we touch and kiss and melt into each other.

Groaning, I adjust myself and try to focus on dinner.

"Everything okay in there? Are you sure you don't want my help?"

Raven's voice floats in the air from where she's lounging on the couch. I picked her up an hour ago and took her grocery shopping. I picked up a few things for tonight while she filled up her cart with her weekly groceries. Raven wasn't too happy that I paid for all of it, but she'll just have to get used to being taken care of.

"All good. The chicken and potatoes just need to sit for a bit," I tell her as I make my way into the living room.

Raven is curled up on my couch, and damn, she looks perfect. Her legs are tucked up underneath her and her black hair is down for once, flowing over her shoulders in luxurious waves. She's holding a sculpture I made a few years back. One of my firsts. I watch her delicate little fingers trace the smooth lines, and suddenly, that's all I want to do to her. Trace her curves, mold her voluptuous body with my hands, map out every inch of her and cover her with kisses.

"Did you make this?" she asks, her voice soft as if she doesn't want to startle me.

I nod, taking a few steps closer until I'm standing right in front of her. Raven looks up at me, stunning me once again with those hazel eyes. She blinks slowly as she studies me, prying me apart and peering into dark places even I'm too scared to look at.

My beautiful goddess reaches out and curls her fingers around my hand, turning over and tracing patterns on my palm with her other hand.

"What are you thinking about, *krolik*?" I whisper.

"How gentle and yet firm your touch must be when you're working with clay," she murmurs more to herself than to me. Then she sears me with a look that's both breathtaking and serious. "You think you're some monster, but that's not what I see. That's not what I've experienced." I don't know what to say, so I just swallow and nod. "Show me more."

"More?" I croak out, swallowing around the lump in my throat.

"Yeah," she says with a sweet, shy smile. My heart speeds up and then stops completely when she looks at me like that. "Do you have a studio or anything?"

"Downstairs," I manage to answer.

"Show me after dinner?"

"Really?"

"Of course!" The excitement in her eyes makes me feel all sorts of confusing emotions.

I close my hand over hers and pull her up, silencing her soft laughter with a kiss. Everything about this woman feels right. I hope she feels it, too.

"Dinner," I grunt when she wiggles against me. My dick is already painfully hard, and her rubbing against it isn't helping.

"Fine," she sighs dramatically. "But then I can see your studio?" She looks at me like she knows how big of a deal it is for me to show her this part of me.

"I promise."

The chicken is rather bland and the potatoes are a little undercooked, but Raven doesn't say a word. She's too busy asking me about my job at Watchdog and drawing out information on Logan, Colton, and their women. I can see it now, the six of us sitting around the dinner table, hanging out and enjoying each other's company. I never could have imagined my life would turn out this way. I didn't even know I wanted that, but with Raven, I want it all.

Raven stands and starts clearing off the plates, but I loop my fingers around her wrist and pull her toward me until she's standing between my legs. Her hands come to my shoulders and I grip her hips, pulling her even closer. She's so damn short we're almost eye level like this. It makes me want to wrap her up in my arms and never let her go.

"Ready?" she asks quietly, licking her bottom lip. I lean forward and place a kiss there before nodding my head. Raven knows I'm showing her so much more than my studio. I'm ripping my goddamn heart out and handing it over to her.

I lead us downstairs, turning the lights on as I go. When I get to the bottom of the stairs, I step to the side, letting Raven have free reign of the place. It's hers now. Everything I own, everything I've built, everything I am is hers.

"Slater..." her voice trails off as she steps further into the room.

I watch her observing my space. Her kaleidoscope eyes take everything in, from the homemade kiln in the corner with its custom ventilation system to the lumps of raw clay covered in rags to keep them the right consistency.

Raven takes her time studying everything, including the unfinished sculpture sitting in the middle of my workbench. "What's this going to be?"

I step up behind her, wrapping my arms around her waist and pulling her against me. "I didn't know until right now," I whisper into the shell of her ear. Raven shivers and relaxes more into me like she can't get enough of my touch.

"What do you mean?"

I slide my hands up her sides, memorizing every curve and dip until I'm cupping her breasts. She moans so sweetly for me and grinds her ass against my thickness. "I want to memorialize your flawless body," I growl softly. "I want to sculpt these curves," I groan, kneading her soft flesh as I suck on her neck.

"Me?" Raven breathes out.

"Yes. You. My little *krolik*. You will be my greatest work of art. Will you let me?"

"N-now? I'm not dressed for it."

I chuckle darkly and kiss her neck again before nibbling on her earlobe. "You don't need clothes, baby girl. I need to see these curves up close. Need to feel them beneath my fingers. Need to see you naked and on display for me."

"Slater..."

I cup her chin and turn her toward me, crashing my lips down on hers. She opens up for me, welcoming my assault. My tongue lashes out against hers, drinking her down and begging her silently to let me have all of her.

Raven turns around in my arms, breaking our kiss. I growl at her, then fall completely silent as she slowly lifts her shirt over her head. I watch with rapt attention as it falls to the ground behind her. And then her hands fiddle with the front of her lacy red bra, unclasping it and letting her breasts spill free.

"Fuck," I grunt, my hands immediately surrounding her gorgeous flesh, squeezing and pinching, and then sucking one pebbled nipple into my mouth. "Perfect," I groan into her skin, trailing little love bites up her neck. "Need to see it all, Raven. Show me what's mine."

She takes a step back, her fingers playing with the waistband of her slacks. My mouth waters and my cock throbs painfully against the zipper of my jeans. As much as I want to tear her clothes off, I want Raven to have this moment. She's giving herself to me, revealing herself inch by inch for my pleasure. Fuck if that doesn't make me feel like the king of the world.

When she's down to just her panties, I stop her. Raven looks up at me, her eyes mostly purple in the soft glow of the scattered light in the basement. "Let me," I whisper, trailing my fingers down her torso and then dipping just the tips into her waistband.

Raven nods, her eyes never leaving mine. I slip my hand into the fabric, cupping her pussy and groaning at how fucking wet she is.

"Oh, God," she whimpers, her breath catching in her throat.

I growl and take her lips in mine as I stroke her and tease out more sexy sounds. Raven rubs herself against me, her hips rocking back and forth like she can't help herself. Her legs shake and she holds her breath, so damn close I can feel her walls pulse around my finger as I thrust in and out of her.

Right before she succumbs to her orgasm, I withdraw my hand and lift her up, setting her on the work table right next to the unfinished sculpture. Raven pouts, but I just grin at her before gripping her thighs and spreading them wide open for me.

"Raven," I groan, sliding my hands up her thighs, stomach, and breasts. I rest my hands on the sides of her neck, stroking her cheeks with my thumbs. "So fucking gorgeous, baby girl. I could get lost in this. In you. Fuck," I growl, squeezing her throat slightly as I lean in and capture her lips once more. I can't seem to stay away from her for one goddamn second.

When we break apart, I step away from her, uncovering the mound of clay. I already have the basic shape of a person, though I had no plan after that. Now that my muse is here, it's time to get started.

I work the clay, kneading the cool material with my hands the same way I kneaded Raven's generous curves. My woman leans back on her hands, still completely naked and on display for me. I stop what I'm doing to run a hand down her neck, between her breasts, and then slip two fingers into her slit, massaging her sensitive bundle of nerves.

"Mmm," she breathes out, spreading her legs wider for me. I attach my lips to her neck, driving her crazy while I work her right up to the edge.

A pained sound escapes her when I pull my hand away before she reaches her peak. I smile against her lips, then weigh her heavy breasts in my hands, swiping my thumbs over her hardened nipples.

Releasing my hold on her, I chuckle when she gasps and pouts. I go back to the clay, rounding out the shape of her breasts and pinching it to form her nipples. I wipe my thumb beneath one breast on the clay model and then the other, shaping them just right.

Looking over at my woman, I nearly come in my damn jeans. She's spread out on the table, leaning back on her elbows as if she's too turned on and wired to do anything else. Her legs are trembling, her sweet juices dripping down onto the table. Raven's hair is a mess and her cheeks are flushed. Her swollen lips call out to me, and when she darts her little tongue out, I snap.

"Mine," I growl, scooping her up into my arms. Raven squeals and then giggles as I drop her down on the bed on the far side of the room. Sometimes I sleep down here if I get inspired or have a bad night and need to work on something to occupy my mind.

I stare down at my breathtaking woman, her eyes sparkling with lust and something else. Something resembling adoration. I don't deserve any of that from her, but I'm selfish and need it anyway.

Crawling on top of her, I gather her hands up in one of mine and pin them above her head. With my other hand, I tuck some of her hair silky black behind her ear, then let my fingertips trail down her jaw, the side of her neck, her collarbone, until I lay my hand right over her heart. I can feel it thundering in her chest, giving away her nerves.

"You're perfect," I whisper, my lips barely touching hers. "Every single part of you. Every dip and curve, every inch of your soft skin." My hand trails lower, the pad of my thumb rubbing light, teasing circles over her nipple. Raven arches her back, shoving her tits further into my hand. I don't think she's even aware she's doing it, which makes my cock swell up almost painfully.

"Slater," Raven moans softly. My lips follow the same path as my fingers, peppering her skin with lingering, open mouthed kisses. When I get to her breasts, I look up at my beautiful girl, capturing her gaze. Our eyes lock, and I never look away as I slowly drag my tongue over her hardened nipple. "Slater!" she cries out, a jolt of electricity shooting through her body.

I groan, wrapping my lips around her tight little peak and sucking. Hard. "These tits are perfect," I growl, palming her other breast and pinching her nipple. She squirms beneath me, spreading her legs and grinding her hot little pussy against my angry, aching cock. "We fit, baby. We fit together. Don't you feel it?"

"Show me," she whispers, almost too softly for me to hear. I look up, training my eyes on hers. Raven nibbles on the corner of her lip, her cheeks turning bright red.

"Are you sure you're ready for that?"

She immediately nods her head, her thighs trembling and tightening around me. "Unless...unless you're not—"

"I am," I growl, taking her lips in a claiming kiss. "I've been ready since I first saw you, Raven. I wanted to bend you over the reception desk and fuck into that tight little pussy from behind until you drenched my cock with your release. I want to give you every kind of pleasure with my fingers, my tongue, my hard as fuck dick." I pause, my features tense as I realize what I just said. It's scandalous, the filthy things I uttered to her. She doesn't look offended, though. If anything, my woman looks even hungrier than before. "I need you to know this is forever," I whisper, reigning in the possessive thoughts. "Right here, you and me. We're forever."

"Really?" she asks on a quiet, shaky breath. The doubt in her voice twists me up inside.

"Yes, *krolik*."

She doesn't say anything, she just stares at me. I see the moment she gives in. The moment she lets go of the last doubt and surrenders herself to what's happening here.

"Show me," Raven says, her hazel eyes pleading with me to prove my words.

Leaning back on my heels, I let go of her wrists so I can slide my hands down her naked body. I trail my lips up the inside of her right leg, pausing briefly to kiss behind her knee. Raven inhales sharply, making me grin wickedly at how well I can read her. I continue placing featherlight kisses up her thigh, nuzzling into her soaking wet pussy.

"Jesus," I groan, unable to resist the urge to lick her from bottom to top. My girl is fucking delicious and I'll never get enough of her.

"More," she whimpers. "I need more. I need it all."

I growl into her cunt, then scrape my teeth along her clit. She lifts her hips and spreads her legs wider. I press my tongue against her tight as fuck entrance, groaning when I feel her little hole pulse and release a shot of cream into my mouth.

Raven lets out a pained cry as she rubs her cunt against my face, coating me in her juices. That's my tipping point. Knowing she marked me, that she's as desperate and needy as I am, and that I'm the only one who can satisfy her, has me tearing at my clothes, desperate to feel all of her with all of me.

My greedy girl whimpers and reaches out for me as I crawl up her sexy as fuck body. I groan when her delicate fingers trail over my shoulders, my chest, my abs, then lower. Resting my forehead on hers, I hiss out a breath when she wraps her hand around my cock and strokes me up and down.

"Fuck, baby girl. You feel so good. So damn good." I let her touch me and explore what now belongs to her. She shocks the hell out of me by guiding me to her entrance and rocking her hips. My eyes snap open, and I groan when I see her gaze burning with lust.

"Slater?" she asks tentatively, her voice not matching up to the pent-up need in her eyes.

"Yeah, baby?"

"I'm...I'm a virgin."

I knew she was, but damn, I like hearing those words on her lips. "I fucking love that I'm your first. It's been years since I've been with anyone. Damn near fifteen. Nothing has ever felt like this, Raven. No one has ever been this important to me. Do you trust me?"

"With all of me," she says with a nod. I close my eyes and let her words wash over me. She wiggles her hips, making us both groan.

"Need me to show you what it means to be mine, bunny?"

"Yes," she whispers. Her eyes are blazing, barely containing the raging fire within.

I push just the tip of my thickness inside her tight as fuck hole. Her pussy spasms, massaging the head of my cock. "Need me to show you how perfectly we'll fit together?" I ask, pushing in just a little further.

"Please," she moans, her fingers curling around my biceps as she spreads her legs open wider for me.

"Need me to make this pussy come? Need me to fill you up so you can fucking come all over me again and again?"

"Yes!" Raven cries out, thrusting her hips up, taking more of me.

I grunt and pull out, swallowing down her whimpers before shoving my cock all the way inside of her tight little channel. I tear through her virginity, growling in feral satisfaction at claiming this woman as mine for all eternity.

"That's it," I soothe her, though all I want to do is rut into her wet heat.

"Slater," Raven moans as her pussy flutters around me, coating me with more of her cream.

I pull out, looking down between us as I set a steady pace. "Look at us, Raven. Fucking look at your little pussy stretching around me, taking my cock like a good girl." I don't know where these words are coming from, but I can't keep them in my head. She doesn't seem to mind.

Raven whimpers and squeezes her inner muscles, making me growl as every part of my dick throbs in torturous pleasure. "More," she cries out, her lips seeking mine. She totally owns this kiss, nipping at me and sucking my tongue inside her mouth as her pussy sucks my cock deeper, deeper, so damn deep.

I pull out and slam back inside her, swallowing down her cries. God, I can feel her channel stretch and clench around me as I pick up speed. Her legs wrap around my torso, her heels digging into my ass, urging me on.

"Fuck, Raven. I don't want to hurt you," I grit out, though I don't slow down. Not for a second. I keep hammering into her over and over, tilting my hips and scraping my cock along her front wall in search of...

"Slater!" Raven shouts and claws at my back, clinging to me as I tear her apart. I can't stop. I know I should slow down, but I don't have control over anything anymore. My hands slip under her back and slide up, my fingers curling around her shoulders, giving me more leverage to fuck that tight little pussy.

Every time I hit the end of her, Raven jerks beneath me, letting out the sexiest whimper. I keep pounding into her as I bury my face into the side of her neck, sucking on her soft skin. I feel her entire body tighten around me, her muscles tensing, her pussy throbbing, pulsing, gushing for me.

I grunt with each savage stroke, more beast than man at the moment. I feel her breaking apart for me, her jagged cries and desperate moans growing louder by the second. She bows her back and digs her fingernails into my shoulders, sucking in a huge breath of air. Raven freezes, tenses, trembles...

And then fucking shatters so beautifully for me.

Her cries of pleasure echo around the room as her cunt snaps around me over and over. I sit back and grip her hips, fucking myself with her spasming pussy. Snow fists the comforter and thrashes her head back and forth as another orgasm rips through her body, leaving her breathless.

"Goddamn," I snarl, shoving my cock deep inside her and staying still. I tip my head back and feel, just fucking feel every ounce of her pleasure ripple around me.

She's still twitching and whimpering out the last of her release when I pull out of her and grab my dick, stroking myself roughly. The need to mark her is such a primal, caveman thing, but it can't be denied. It won't.

My orgasm slams into me, and I roar as I paint her tits and pussy with my cum. I grunt something unintelligible, squeezing my dick so damn hard as it jerks and empties more of my release all over her.

I'm about to collapse, but then my dirty fucking girl rubs my seed into her skin. I crave more of her. I already know I'll never get enough.

Sliding down her body, I pry her legs open. Flattening my tongue, I lick her up and down in frantic, feral strokes before spearing my tongue inside her entrance, scooping out more of her cream.

Raven winds her fingers in my hair, holding me still as she rubs her pussy against my lips and tongue. Her scream carves through the air as a fierce orgasm overwhelms her fully, curvy body. I grip her thighs, pinning them down to the mattress as I drink down every last drop of her release.

I only stop when she goes completely limp. Looking up from between her legs, I see her head loll to the side as her chest heaves up and down. I crawl up her body, placing kisses on her stomach, her breasts, her neck, and finally her lips.

Collapsing beside her, I drape my precious Raven over my chest and hold her trembling body close. We're both breathing heavily, our bodies slick with sweat as we cling to each other. I comb my fingers through her damp hair and place a kiss on top of her head.

"You okay, *krolik*?" I whisper, tugging on her hair slightly to tilt her head up.

"Hmm?" she asks in a daze, her eyelids barely fluttering open as a sleepy, contented smile stretches across her lips.

I grin and kiss the tip of her nose. "Never mind. I've got you," I murmur, tucking her head under my chin. I hold her for long moments, listening to her breaths slowly return to normal.

Eventually, I get up and lift my woman into my arms, smiling when she curls into me and tucks her head between my neck and shoulder. I carry her to my bedroom, tucking her in before curling around her.

She's incredible. I don't deserve her, but she's mine now. I just hope I don't fuck it up.

Chapter 8

Raven

Something shatters the dark silence of the night, ripping me from my sleep. My heart is racing, making my temples throb as I blink awake.

"No!" A raw, agonizing growl sounds from the other side of the bed. Slater thrashes, turning on his side to face me.

My breath catches in my throat when I look at his face. Slater is still sleeping, his mind lost in some horrible memory. Sweat beads on his forehead as his eyebrows pull tight with tension. I reach out to wake him up, but Slater catches my hand, his eyes snapping open.

His blue eyes are nearly black, but that's not what concerns me. Slater's face is blank, completely void of emotion as he stares right through me. I can tell the nightmare is still gripping him, and it makes tears burn the back of my eyes. What has my giant teddy bear been through in his life that left him with these kinds of night terrors?

Slater flips me on my back. I gasp as he looms over me, taking in the scared, threatened, hurt beast he's become.

"Come back to me, Slater," I whisper, looking him straight in the eye. "It's over. Whatever has a hold of you is in the past." I'm well aware this could end horribly, but it's painful watching Slater go through this. How many nights has he spent tossing and turning, trying to escape the clutches of the past? My heart breaks for him.

Reaching out with my free hand, I cup his face. Slater clenches his jaw and snarls, but I keep my hand there, stroking his stubble and telling him he's safe.

Slater blinks rapidly and gains control of himself once more. He looks down at me, then up at my wrist, where he's pinning it to the bed. Slater rolls off of me and jumps out of bed before I can even take a breath.

"Dammit," he mutters, scrubbing his hands down his face.

I follow him, both of us naked in the moonlight streaming through the window. "Slater," I murmur, putting my hand on his forearm. He jerks away from me and I stumble back a bit before catching myself.

"Fuck," he growls, reaching out for my shoulders to steady me. "Fuck, I'm sorry," he exhales, not looking me in the eye. "Are you okay? Did I... Did I..." Slater drops his hands from me and looks away. "Did I hurt you?" His voice is so broken, so full of shame.

"No, I'm fine," I assure him. "But what about you? What happened to give you such horrible nightmares?"

Slater turns, giving me his back. He's shutting me out. My heart sinks, not only because I want him to trust me, but because he's been carrying the weight of whatever happened all alone for so long.

"I'm sorry," he says again. "I could have... fuck, I would never forgive myself if—"

"But you didn't," I insist, knowing exactly where this spiral is leading.

"But I could have. In that state of mind, I'm capable of anything," he whispers, his words dripping with shame.

"You wouldn't hurt me," I say softly, approaching Slater as if he's a wounded animal. "And if you did, well, I'd kick your ass."

Slater pauses, then finally faces me. He looks so weary, yet I see him hiding a little smirk. "Oh yeah, little bunny? You're going to kick my ass?"

"Yup," I nod, giving him a smile.

He reaches out for me, then freezes before dropping his hands at his sides. I'm not having any of that, though. I wrap my arms around Slater, burying myself in his embrace. Every muscle in his body tenses, but he relaxes the longer I hold him.

Finally, Slater wraps his arms around me and kisses the top of my head. "I'm so sorry," he whispers over and over again.

I press a kiss to the center of his chest, then lean back, taking his hand in mine. "Come back to bed. Tell me about what haunts you."

Slater looks down at our entwined fingers and then back up at me. "Do you trust me?"

He nods and squeezes my hand, leading us back to the bed. I crawl in, followed by Slater. I'm about to turn around to face him, but Slater wraps an arm around my waist and pulls me closer, so he's spooning around me. His body engulfs mine, cocooning me in his warmth and strength. I somehow know this is the only way he'll talk to me. It would be too much, too vulnerable to look me in the eye while he's spilling his heart out.

"Before Logan, Colton, and I started Watchdog, we were all Marines," Slater begins. I nod my head and place my hand over his where he's holding my stomach. "They got out, but I stayed. I was going to be a lifer. But then..."

He sighs heavily and I resist the urge to turn around and cradle the giant of a man in my arms. "I'm right here," I whisper. "I'm not going anywhere." Something tells me he needed to hear that.

"I was overseas, riding with a few people from my unit. We were headed to the nearest village to grab some decent food when we ran over a roadside bomb."

"Oh my God," I gasp, tears spilling down my cheeks. Slater tightens his hold on me, burying his face into the back of my neck. His next words are muffled.

"I'm the only one left."

It takes a second for me to comprehend what he said. When it finally clicks, squeeze his hand and turn to look at him over my shoulder. "And you regret it?" I whisper. Slater doesn't say anything. His silence tells me everything I need to know. "Slater, I'm so sorry you've experienced that kind of loss and devastation. I can't even begin to understand what that's like to go through or what it's like to deal with the aftermath."

He takes a shuddering breath and kisses my temple. "It fucked me up, Raven. A piece of me will always be missing. You deserve someone who can give you everything. All of them."

"I don't want anyone else," I say with determination. "I want you. I want all the pieces you're willing to give me."

"You can't," he whispers. "You can't want me."

"Too late."

I feel his lips pull into a small smile against the back of my neck before he places a kiss there. "I don't deserve you."

"You deserve to be seen and loved."

Slater inhales sharply, and I realize what I said. Do I love him? Of course. It feels like I always have. But I don't know if he's ready to hear that. Instead of pressing the issue, I decide to show him how much he means to me.

Slater kisses my neck again and I melt into him, rubbing myself against his already hard length. Slater groans but doesn't go any further. I can't explain it. My body wants him so badly. I need to comfort him and show him I'm not afraid to surrender to him. I move his hand that's around my waist up to cup my breast.

He groans, massaging my sensitive skin. "Are you sure?" Slater growls, his swollen cock already throbbing against my ass.

"I need you as much as you need me," I promise, grinding against his growing erection.

Slater growls and kisses my neck again. His hand slides under the covers, finding my legs and sliding his finger up my slit, causing me to buck against him. "So wet for me. You have no idea how much I want you right now," he groans into my skin before sucking and licking my neck.

I moan as he dips one finger into my entrance and grinds his palm down on my clit. My breath catches in my throat as he continues to pump in and out of me, adding another finger.

"Mmm, please, Slater, I need you inside me," I moan. Where this wanton woman came from, I have no idea.

"Anything for you, baby girl."

Slater pushes the blankets down and lifts my top leg up over his hip. His cock slides in and out of my wet slit, not entering me just yet. He gathers up my juices, bumping over my clit in the most delicious way with each thrust.

When I'm on the edge of combustion, Slater pulls back and thrusts deep inside of me, causing me to cry out.

"So fucking good," he grunts.

He starts off with long, slow thrusts, hitting the end of me each time. He's dragging this out. I was ready to explode, but he's bringing me back down. I'm frustrated but in the best way possible. I trust him to take care of me, pleasure me, and meet my needs.

When he slides his hand down my tummy and starts rubbing my clit, I almost lose it.

"Jesus, Raven. I feel your pussy squeezing me."

"Yes, God yes, please, more..."

He pistons in and out of me while blurring his fingers over my clit and kissing my neck. I love that he knows just how to handle my body, how to bring me to the brink, how to push me over into the most exquisite kind of pain and pleasure.

"Slater, ohmygod, Slater!"

"That's it. I feel you. I feel your need for release. Give it to me. Let go, Raven."

His words throw me over the edge as I tremble and gasp out my orgasm. Slater pulls out and flips me on my back, entering me again in one hard thrust. I'm still coming, my cunt pulses around him, trying to suck him back into me.

Slater comes down to his forearms, resting one on either side of my head. He looks over my face and then kisses me, slow and deep, while rocking himself in and out of me. My legs wrap around his hips, urging him deeper. He pulls my bottom lip in between his teeth, causing me to moan and throw my head back, exposing my neck to him.

I feel his teeth, tongue, and lips devouring the tender skin of my neck. Slater sits back slightly, taking my hands in his, lacing our fingers together, and pulling them above my head as he pounds into me.

"Fuck. Love watching those tits shake for me. You're so beautiful. So goddamn beautiful."

My muscles tense, my back bows off the mattress, and my nails dig into the back of Slater's hands, as I feel my body brace for another orgasm.

Slater feels it too. He fucks me so, so deep, as I climb higher than I ever thought possible. I keep thinking I'm going to snap, but each thrust winds me up tighter, pushing my body to the absolute limit. Slater pulls all the way out and slams into me one last time. I come. *Hard.* His mouth covers mine, swallowing my screams as I thrash and squeeze and release over and over again.

He swells up inside of me and hot liquid squirts into my pussy. Slater growls and continues to pump into me, prolonging both of our orgasms.

When we are both spent, he rolls on his back and drags me over his chest.

"Thank you," he murmurs softly, brushing the hair away from my face.

"I'm right here whenever you need me," I promise.

Slater holds me for long moments, trailing a hand up and down my spine in soothing strokes. "Sleep now, *krolik*." He kisses the top of my head and plays with my hair until darkness clouds my vision and I fall asleep wrapped up in Slater.

***

Twelve hours ago, I was in heaven. I woke up with Slater wrapped around me, his wintergreen scent mixed with the remnants of our lovemaking last night.

I had hoped we could get breakfast and then go into the library together, but something was off. He still kissed me and made me coffee, but he looked... sad. When he told me he had to check in with his co-workers at Watchdog headquarters, I thought maybe he was just disappointed that we wouldn't be spending that time together.

But then he didn't show up to his shift.

Instead, some guy named Ryan showed up. He seems nice enough, but he's not Slater. When I casually asked why they switched it up, Ryan just shrugged and said the bosses were off on a special case.

That was right before lunch. I skipped my leftovers in the fridge since I felt like I was going to throw up. Slater didn't leave me... right? We shared something amazing, and it wasn't just sex. He opened up to me, showed me his studio, told me about his nightmares, and bared his beautiful, broken soul to me. How can he walk away from that? I get that he probably feels vulnerable right now, but so am I, dammit!

"Ugh," I sigh, drawing out the sound until I don't have any air left in my lungs. There's no one around to hear me being dramatic, so I sigh loudly again. It feels strangely cathartic.

Looking at the clock on the wall, I see it's almost seven-thirty. We've been closing the library early for the last few weeks, so I'm the only one here. I assume Ryan is still here, but I guess I never told him I was staying late. Truthfully, I lost track of time. As much as I despise data entry and budget sheets, they do provide a good distraction.

When I can no longer avoid going home, I pack up my stuff and shut off the light to my office.

"Oh shoot," I gasp, realizing all the other lights are off in the building. Maybe Ryan is outside waiting for me to lock up.

Turning on the flashlight on my phone, I light the path to the back door. The hairs on my neck and arms stand up, making my skin prickle with awareness. I'm sure it's just the dark. I've never liked the dark, even less now with my father's men on my tail.

"I'm fine," I whisper, taking another cautious step forward.

Placing one foot in front of the other, I keep walking toward the back door, praying Ryan is still there. Maybe I can ask him to walk me home since it's only a few blocks. My stomach twists, thinking about Slater. If he were here, he'd insist I go home on time. Or maybe he'd insist I go home with him.

Then where the heck is he? Why did he seem so sad this morning? Why didn't he show up for his shift?

I'm lost in my thoughts when I hear a loud clap. One of the windows rattles as if something blunt was thrown at it. I squeak and run to the back door, flinging it open and running outside.

Inhaling deeply, I bend down and rest my hands on my knees. It's then I see Ryan. On the ground. With his hands tied and his face bloodied.

I snap my head up, darting my eyes around. I'm frozen in place. I should run back inside, and—

"There you are, bitch," someone grunts. I hear them clear the phlegm from their throat and then spit on the ground.

Turning around slowly, my eyes meet Paul's. I'm no match for him. He's at least a foot taller than me and has tightly packed muscles hidden under a few layers of fat. He's hefty, but I know from experience he's strong and ruthless.

With no other weapons on hand, I swing my canvas bag full of the latest sci-fi trilogy I checked out today. It hits him square in the chest, making him stumble backward and force out a breath.

I open my mouth to scream for help, but he covers my entire face with his hand and shoves me backward, toward a van with blackout windows. I shake my head, trying to free his hold on me, but he spins me around and locks my hands behind my back with one of his.

Paul pushes me roughly, and I let out a pained sound when my arm twists in his hold.

"Shut up!" he roars, grabbing the back of my neck with his free hand.

Paul walks me up to the vehicle and is about to toss me inside when he pauses. I stiffen in his hold, then look straight ahead, into the black, reflective windows of the van. Relief floods through me when I see the reflection.

Slater is here to rescue me.

Chapter 9

Slater

"Get your fucking filthy hands off of her," I roar as I grab the back of his jacket and throw the dead motherfucker on the ground.

"What the—"

I cut him off with a kick to the ribs, then turn to face Raven. Her eyes are filled with tears and she's barely able to take a breath. "Get back," I warn her, my voice almost feral. I can't help it. I have so much pent-up rage and I'm trying to focus it on the dumbass who thought he could hurt Raven.

She gasps and scrambles away, hiding in the shadows. It's then I notice Ryan, my apparently worthless replacement. He's tied up and passed out, though it looks like it only took one good blow to the head to do it. Weak.

When I snap my attention back to the large man on the ground, red swirls in my vision. He stops squirming, and black, hooded eyes stare back at me. It happens in an instant. He pulls a gun from his jacket and aims at me. I don't think, I just fall on him, knocking the gun out of his hand and crushing him into the cement.

He's a big dude, but I've got six inches and fifty pounds of muscle on him. I slam my forehead against his, grinning with sick satisfaction when his head bounces off the pavement.

Sitting up, I deliver a right hook to his jaw, then bust his nose with another blow. The adrenaline is rushing through me, followed by righteous anger. He thinks he can take Raven and force her into a life she never asked for? He wants to play the big bad kidnapper? I'm more than happy to show him what it's like playing in the big leagues.

I stand up, placing a boot on the center of his chest when he tries to follow. "Raven doesn't belong to you," I spit out, moving my foot up to his neck and pressing down. "And she sure as hell doesn't belong to her father." The dumb fuck's face is turning purple, so I let up. Can't have him passing out on me when he has more to suffer through.

The man coughs and sputters, spitting out blood and two teeth. "I'll go, I'll go," he pleads, holding his hands up in surrender.

"You'll go and tell your employer that Raven is her own person and she gets to choose her life. You'll tell him if he continues to send men after her, I won't go easy on them like I have with you."

"Easy?" he squeaks out, no doubt feeling every one of his broken bones and wounds.

"I'm letting you live so you can send a warning. The next fool they send my way won't be so lucky."

"Yes, yes, I'll tell them. I'll tell them anything," he rambles.

I look him over one last time, satisfied for now with his injuries. When I notice the bastard has peed his pants, I grin and pull him off the ground. I get right in his face, close enough to smell his fear. "Now get the fuck out of here before I change my mind."

The man stumbles and falls on his ass before scrambling up and limping toward the van. I take note of the license plate, which I'll look up later.

Taking a deep breath, I flex every muscle, willing the rage back down to the dark core of me where it belongs. My knuckles are bruised and I have blood splatters on my arms and clothes. I'm a monster. A monster who doesn't deserve someone as pure as Raven. My little bunny.

I can't look at her. Shame coils deep in my chest, tightening and squeezing the air out of my lungs. I should have been here sooner. Then he wouldn't have had a chance to touch her at all. Fuck, I should have been here, period.

Colton's girl was in danger and we, along with Logan, had to go scope out the situation. What a goddamn day. We faced down a mafia reject, and now I'm taking out more trash. I should have come in for the rest of my shift, but I didn't have it in me to face Raven.

She said she wasn't afraid of me last night, that she trusted me. That's a mistake. Clearly. I can't defeat the demons in my head, what made me think I could protect someone as precious as Raven?

I rub my temples, trying to ward off memories of the bomb. I couldn't save them. I couldn't get there fast enough. I still can't face my shame, which is why it haunts me in my sleep. I'm too fucked up. I'm good for muscle and not much else. Certainly not good enough to have Raven's trust.

A soft hand on my back pulls me from my thoughts. I can't turn around. I can't look at her, otherwise, I might break. Raven wraps her arms around me from behind, burying her face into my back. Longing and lust rocket through me, but I can't give in.

Then my sweet girl shudders out a sob, clinging to me even tighter. I can't stand her tears. Slowly, I turn around, cupping her face in my hands. Her hazel eyes are round and glossy from crying, her little nose tipped in red. Raven's bottom lip trembles, and that's all I can take.

I wrap her up in my arms, pressing her against me. She sinks into my embrace, snuggling closer even though I'm covered in sweat and blood.

"You're h-here," she sniffles.

I nod and grunt, unable to form words around the lump in my throat.

"I knew you'd come."

Her words are my undoing.

I step away from her, getting ready to call Logan to pick Raven up. I know she'll be safe with Logan and his woman, Spencer. Plus, Spencer will be thrilled to have a new friend. It's what's best.

Raven shocks me by jumping up and looping her arms around my neck. I catch her and press her up against my body, savoring her soft curves one last time.

"I have to let you go," I murmur, even as I bury my nose in her hair.

"No," she says forcefully.

"No?"

Raven loosens her hold on me and I slide her down my body until her feet touch the ground. She places one hand on my cheek, keeping me close, while her other hand covers my heart. Those ethereal eyes capture mine and don't let go. Blues swirl with greens and browns, each color pulling me deeper into her spell. I swear the purple rings around her eyes glow as she sets her jaw and puffs out her chest. She looks like she's about to yell at me, which is exactly what I deserve.

"You said I'm my own person and I get to choose my life. I choose you, Slater. Every time, I'll choose you. I just want to love you. Why won't you let me?"

Her voice wobbles at the end, showing me how hard it is for her to stand up for herself. Is she really afraid of losing me? She should want me gone after the nightmare last night, the rough way I handled her, and now failing to protect her.

"I don't des—"

"Nope. That's not a good reason. It's bullshit and we both know it."

I grin. I can't help it. She's so determined, so sexy, so sure of herself in this moment. More than that, she's sure of *me*. "Raven," I whisper, closing my eyes and resting my forehead on hers. "I've failed you so many times already."

"Stop, Slater. Stop blaming yourself for the bomb. Stop blaming yourself for the toll it's taken on you. And definitely stop blaming yourself for last night or today."

"But—"

She covers my mouth with her hand, shocking a laugh right out of me. My feisty woman. She's certainly not afraid of me, which is a relief.

"Haven't you suffered enough?" she whispers. "Isn't it tiring, carrying around this shame that was never yours in the first place?"

Once again, Raven's words strike at the very core of who I am. All I know is shame and penance. What would my life be without them?

One look into those captivating, mesmerizing eyes, and I know. Her. Raven. My *krolik*.

"I'm sorry," I choke out, blinking away tears. I haven't cried in... fuck, two decades? Three?

"I'm only accepting apologies for not talking to me before you got caught up in your head," Raven says with a playful yet tentative smile. "Promise we'll always talk. Even about the hard stuff. Especially about the hard stuff. Slater, I—"

"I love you," I blurt out, needing to say it first.

"Hey," she pouts. "I was going to say that."

I nip at her bottom lip, then kiss my woman, sealing our promises and declarations.

My phone buzzes in my pocket, breaking us apart. I'm about to throw the damn thing against the wall and get back to Raven, but Logan's name pops up on the screen.

"Slater, did you check-in at the library? Ryan said—"

"Ryan failed to stop the threat and he'll be fired as soon as he wakes up," I growl.

There's silence on the other end of the line, then Logan takes a deep breath. "Is everyone okay?"

I look down at Raven, who nods. "Yes. Thank fuck."

"What a day," Logan mutters, the exhaustion heavy in his voice.

"Agreed. Get some rest, man. I'll take care of Raven."

"Raven, huh?"

"Shut it," I grunt. Raven giggles, which makes Logan laugh.

"I'm happy for you. Truly."

"Yeah, yeah, thanks. We're going home. We'll deal with the rest tomorrow and I'll get you up to speed on what happened. Everything's okay for now."

After hanging up, I lift Raven into my arms and hold her close while I stomp through the parking lot to my SUV. She lets me buckle her in, even kissing me on the cheek when I bend over to click her seatbelt in place. I'm still not sure I deserve her sweetness, but after the way she declared her love for me, I know I have to try. She wants me? I'm all fucking hers.

"Would you like to take a warm bath?" I ask Raven once we're inside my house. *Our* house. There's no way I'm letting her go back to her apartment.

"You have a bathtub?"

I pull her toward me, kissing the top of her head. I can't get enough of these little touches. The fight and adrenaline are draining away, leaving me with the reality of what could have happened if I didn't show up in time.

"I use it to soak my leg or shoulder when they start to hurt," I whisper. Admitting my weaknesses is still hard, but I know Raven will accept me as I am.

"So it's a pretty massive tub, huh?" She giggles at her own joke. Fucking adorable.

"It'll fit both of us if that's what you're asking." Her eyes go wide and her cheeks flush that pretty pink color I love so much. Raven nods her head and nibbles on her bottom lip, and I groan at the eager look on her face. "Not tonight, baby girl. You need rest."

Raven pouts and then lets out a huge yawn. I smirk, kissing the tip of her nose before leading her down the hall to the bathroom.

After she's settled in and has a shirt and boxers of mine to change into, I step out and go to the basement where I have a shower set up in the corner. I rinse off the blood and dirt, scrubbing away the anger and fear until all that's left is love for my little *krolik*.

She's still relaxing in the tub by the time I'm out of the shower and dressed. I sit down on the couch, then hop up, pacing around the living room. I can feel the restlessness settling in, the doubts crawling around in my head and trying to poison my thoughts.

I take out my phone and do something I haven't done since I got out of the military three years ago. I call my brother, Hudson.

"Slater? Is everything okay?"

I'm not surprised that's his first reaction. Why else would I be calling unless it was an emergency? Truthfully, I have no fucking clue either. I just wanted to hear someone's voice who isn't in the middle of all this. Logan and Colton are all hopped up on love, and while I'm growing to appreciate the rose-colored glasses, I want someone else to talk to. That's what family is for, right? I wouldn't know. I've been an absent brother, son, and grandson for years.

"Slater?"

"Yeah," I cough out. Clearing my throat, I try again. "I'm fine. I just... fuck." I rub the back of my neck and try to figure out what to say.

"I'm glad you called," Hudson jumps in. "It's good to hear your voice."

I grunt, making him chuckle. Hudson was also in the military, but he recently left after a few tours and moved back to our hometown of Rosewood, Colorado.

"How are... things?" I ask. I'm awkward as fuck, but for some reason, I want to make this connection with family again. Maybe it's because I want Raven to have a family, too. Her worthless parents don't count.

"Rosewood is the same as always," he says easily, taking the burden of conversation off my shoulders. "I'm running The Pink Door now. Or, at least I'm the owner on paper. Grams is never far away, giving her input on every detail."

I grin at the reminder of our grandmother. Connie Wolf has a big heart and an even bigger mouth. That woman loves to be up in everyone's business. She also loves to gossip.

"No shit? Running the family tavern? Are you going to change the color and name? You've always hated the obnoxious pink door."

Hudson sighs, and I can almost picture him pacing around his room, just like I'm doing right now. "Well, about that. I'm hiring an interior designer. Or, well, I'm trying to." He sounds frustrated.

"Trying to?"

"She's being difficult."

"The designer?" It sounds like there's more to the story.

"Yes. To be fair, I can't stop making a fool of myself every time I see her. First, I accidentally kicked her out of the bar."

"Accidentally?"

"Yeah, well, Grams was involved, so there's that."

"Uh-huh," I chuckle.

"Then I embarrassed her and she ran away. And to top it all off, I insulted her profession." The poor guy sounds exasperated. "You don't happen to have any advice for apologizing to women, do you?"

I laugh and wipe a hand down my face. "No fair, I called to ask you for advice about women."

A beat of silence passes, and then Hudson chuckles. The sound is warm and rich, and I've missed it. I've missed Hudson.

"We're a pair, huh? What's going on in your life? You have someone special?" He sounds genuinely happy for me, even after I've ignored him for years.

"Yeah. She's... she's incredible. And for some reason, she wants to be with me."

"Sounds like you don't need advice," he teases.

"What if I fuck it up?" I blurt out.

"Apologize," Hudson deadpans.

"Yeah, and you're so good at that," I mutter. He laughs again, making me smile.

Hudson's voice turns more serious. "I don't know what you've been through the last few years, but if you've found someone who accepts you and makes you happy, nothing else matters. She wants to be with you, you said it yourself. Trust that. Trust her."

I grunt again, considering his words. "Maybe your designer needs to hear that, too. That she can trust you."

"Well, damn. Look who ended up giving solid advice after all!"

"Shut up," I growl, though I'm mostly laughing at this point. I notice movement from the other side of the room, and turn to face Raven, fresh out of the bath and wearing my shirt. "I gotta go."

"Get your girl, Slater."

"You too, Hudson."

"Don't be a stranger, man. It's good talking to you."

"Same."

I hang up and toss the phone on the couch, then prowl toward Raven. The little minx isn't wearing my boxers, which means nothing is covering up her pussy. I told her earlier she needed rest, but that was before she came out here and tempted me.

"You need something from me, baby girl?"

Chapter 10

Raven

Slater stalks toward me like a predator, his dark blue eyes glowing as he looks me up and down. God, he looks hungry. I am, too. I want to hold him while he sinks into me, claiming me the way we both need. I told Slater I loved him, and now I want to prove it to him over and over.

"Always," I say in answer to his question. "I need you."

The intense look in his eyes softens, and all I want is to be swept up in his arms. Slater hears my silent prayer and lifts me off my feet, cradling me close to his chest as he storms off to the bedroom.

Slater tosses me on the bed, looming over me as he looks me up and down. In this moment, he looks absolutely possessed, like a wild animal. Underneath it though, I still see the way he cares for me. I know he'd never hurt me, which makes me want to unlock the beast I know he's trying to suppress.

I lean up to kiss him again, but he pulls away. I strain my neck higher, but he pulls back farther, grinning as I pout. He gives me a chaste kiss and gets off the bed.

I follow him, about to complain, but then I see him take his shirt off, revealing his chest to me. I can't help but lick my lips as my eyes drift over the tattoos swirling over one shoulder and down his chest. Then my eyes drop lower to his six-pack, and lower still, to those two sculpted lines leading to his massive dick.

When I finally drag my eyes back up to meet his, he's smirking at me.

I start to take my shirt off too, but he reaches out, taking my hands in his. He kisses one and then the other, before lifting them above my head. His hands slide down my arms, slowly, burning a path as they go. Slater cups my breasts and keeps moving his hands down over my torso.

Then he grasps the hem of my shirt and lifts it up over my head in one fluid motion.

Staler growls and then kneels down in front of me, kissing a trail down my stomach. At the same time, his hands skim up the back of my legs, and then he pulls me forward so he can kiss my pussy. My inner muscles clench with desire, and I know he sees my juices dripping down the inside of my thighs.

"Goddamn," he groans before leaning down and licking up my arousal. Slater dips his tongue inside of my slit and then pushes me back on the bed, making me squeal.

He spreads my thighs apart and guides one leg over his shoulder, and then the other, opening me up for him. Then, Slater dives into my soaking wet cunt, making me cry out with the feeling of his hot mouth on my most private place.

He begins slowly, with long waves of his tongue that roll up and down inside my pussy. Just when I need more, his thumb finds my clit and rubs circles around the little ball of nerves while he continues to lick me and suck on my folds.

An index finger slides inside of me with ease, then a middle finger joins as he pistons in and out of me with his muscular arm, fucking me into the bed. He rotates his fingers and curls them up, finding that secret spot. He rubs his fingers against it and watches me tense and moan as he completely destroys me with his touch.

"Yes, oh yes," I cry out, unable to stop myself.

He growls into my pussy, making my clit vibrate with his voice. Slater slides and twists and rubs the walls of my pussy with his fingers while his tongue does wicked things to my little bundle of nerves. He licks it, bats it around, and finally sucks it into his mouth and bites down gently, causing my orgasm to rip through me and spill all over his fingers.

I buck my hips as he sticks his tongue in my entrance, lapping up everything I'm giving him.

When I finally come back down to earth, I sink into the mattress. Slater climbs on top of me, propping himself up on one elbow while his other hand cups my face. He presses gentle kisses all over with featherlight touches of his lips. He tickles my forehead, nose, cheeks, and finally, my mouth. Slater strokes his tongue inside of me slowly, deliberately, while his hand moves from my face and trails down my body, caressing me and setting me on fire.

I spread my legs and welcome more of his skin on my skin. At some point, Slater rid himself of his pants and boxers. I feel his hot, hard cock rubbing against my pussy. I wrap my legs around his hips and try to pull him where I need him most.

Slater pushes inside of me, slowly, his eyes never leaving mine. I feel so connected to him, in every single way.

"Breathe for me, baby girl," he whispers before kissing my forehead.

I take a deep breath and stare into those beautiful eyes of his. They are full of emotion, warmth, and love. I truly feel like I'm the most important thing in the world to him right now.

"Slater," I whimper, half from the tender moment we're sharing and half from the impending orgasm that's threatening to tear me in two. "I want to feel you move."

We both groan as he pulls out and hits home over and over. I love feeling the thick veins in his cock sliding against the walls of my pussy as he moves in and out of me.

"So goddamn tight, Jesus, you feel so good, Raven."

"You... too..." I manage to say in between thrusts. I wrap my arms around his back and grip the taut muscles there, clinging to him while he picks up speed.

Slater twists his hips slightly, changing up the angle. He hits that spot inside of me with his dick, making my whole body jerk in his arms.

"Does that feel good?" he asks.

"Y-yes..." I moan.

I dig my nails into his back to spur him on. Slater crashes his mouth down on mine as our bodies come together, again and again, flesh meeting flesh, pleasure meeting pleasure. I squeeze my legs around him and clench my pussy to get him deeper inside of me.

Slater thrusts into me harder, faster, each stroke of his dick pushing me closer, closer, hitting that spot over and over, once, twice, again, again, *fuck*, one more time, please, please, I need it, my body trembling and aching for more.

He slams into me one last time and I scream, shattering around him. My pussy clamps down on his thick cock as all my muscles tense up tightly and then unwind, the orgasm rolling through me in explosive waves.

"That's it, sweetheart, that's so fucking it, come for me again, Raven."

I shake my head, unable to imagine myself doing that again. Slater, however, doesn't take no for an answer. He leans back and sits on his heels, grabbing my hips and fucking himself with my body. The angle is different, deeper, hitting new places that make me shake and moan uncontrollably.

"Oh, God, Slater. This is..."

I gasp and cry out as I feel his fingers blurring over my clit. With one pinch, he has me twisting in his arms, but he won't let me escape the onslaught of sensations as my orgasm claws at me and rips me apart from the inside out. I thrash and scream as Slater continues to fuck me through it.

I open my eyes as my orgasm fades and see him sink into me again and again. It's dirty and hot as hell. His movements become jerky and his thickness grows impossibly larger. He's throbbing and thrusting and working me up into another orgasm, both of us sweating and shaking.

Then he pulls himself out and strokes himself once before spraying his cum all over my tits and stomach.

"Fuck, fuck, fuck, Raven," he groans. "Mine, fucking *mine*."

The next second, Slater is kneeling in between my legs, licking my swollen pussy as he rubs his cum into my skin. The feeling of his hot seed cooling against my skin, his tongue dipping into my entrance, his teeth scraping against my clit, has me bowing my back off the bed and climaxing so hard I can't breathe.

Barely giving me any time to recover, Slater flips me on my stomach and plunges his already hard cock inside of me. Cum coats my thighs as my cunt snaps around his length. He pounds into me mercilessly, making obscene noises as he throws me off the edge into yet another blinding orgasm, sobbing my release. This time, I take him with me, both of us falling into endless pleasure. Slater shoots his load deep inside of me, rope after rope until he is spent.

I must have passed out there for a second because when I open my eyes, Slater has me wrapped up in his arms and he's pressing soft kisses over my face and neck.

"That good, huh?" he whispers, a hint of playfulness in his voice.

"That... cocky... huh?" I gasp out, still catching my breath as I float down to earth.

"Yeah, I suppose my cock deserves some credit too," he laughs.

I narrow my eyes at him, but can't hide my smile. Slater is teasing me, and he looks lighter and happier than I've ever seen him.

"I love you," I say softly.

"Raven, I love you so much. I'm sorry I freaked out and—"

"You already apologized. Do you not believe me when I said I forgive you?" I ask, quirking an eyebrow up.

"I do. It'll take me some time to accept it, I think."

"That's okay. I'll be right here." I yawn and curl up on his chest, loving the way his laughter feels against my cheek.

"You're perfect, you know that? So perfect."

Slater strokes my hair and continues whispering sweet things to me until my breathing evens out and my heart rate slows. I know we need to clean up, but I don't think I can move from this spot. Good thing

Slater isn't in a hurry to get up either. In fact, he snuggles down a little closer and presses a kiss to the top of my head. I don't think there's ever been a more perfect moment.

Chapter 11

The last few weeks have been the best of my life. I still don't believe I deserve the kind of love and joy Raven gives me, but I'm trying real damn hard to trust that she loves me, scars, trauma, and all.

We both took a few days to recover after all the shit that went down at the library. Logan, Colton, and I are keeping tabs on Raven's father and his men, as well as all of his business partners. So far, it looks like they've accepted the fact that Raven is mine and no one else's. I'll be ready if they try to take her from me again.

"Come on, asshole," I mutter to the car in front of me. The little red Honda is going two miles under the speed limit, which is unacceptable. I'm on my way to pick Raven up from the library, and this guy is getting in my way.

Swerving around him, I glare at the driver, only feeling a little guilty that he's about ninety years old.

I pull into the parking lot, growling when I don't see any other cars there. Storming out of my car, I sprint up to the backdoor, which is unlocked. I frown and throw the door open, running inside to find my Raven.

My pulse races and my heart rate kicks up the longer I don't see her. Rounding another corner, I weave in and out of the bookshelves, stopping short when I see the most beautiful sight.

Raven is up on her tiptoes, reaching above her head to put a book away. The sun is just beginning to set, the golden rays silhouetting her full, curvy frame as she stretches her body out.

I growl, causing Raven to look at me over her shoulder. Her hazel eyes sparkle when they catch mine. I'll never understand how she can look at me with such adoration, but I'm thankful for every ounce of affection she gives me.

Turning around, Raven faces me, a seductive smile on her lips.

"You shouldn't be here alone," I grunt, sliding my hands into her hair and tilting her head up. My little vixen licks her lips, making me groan.

"Maybe I wanted you to come find me," she murmurs, her eyes turning dark. I dip my head down to kiss her neck, breathing in her sweet scent and sucking my mark there. "Hey!" she squeals.

I cover her mouth with mine, tasting every inch of her and pressing her against the bookshelf as I deepen our kiss.

"What, exactly, were you hoping would happen, *krolik*?"

Raven's cheeks burn bright red, and my dick twitches as I wait for her to tell me.

"I've always wanted to have sex in a library," she admits softly.

I growl and claim her lips once more, my cock throbbing at her dirty, perfect request. "You want me to fuck you right here, baby girl? Against the bookshelf?"

"Anywhere," she breathes out, rubbing her pussy against me. "Everywhere. God, Slater, I can't get enough of you."

Gripping her hips, I spin her around so she's facing the bookshelf. I nibble on her pulse point and lick away the sting before grazing my lips on the shell of her ear.

"Hands on the shelf, little bunny. Bend over and show me that ass."

Raven moans and bends over, giving me permission to fulfill our deepest desires. I pull down her pants and frilly white panties so they are around her knees, then smooth my hands over the soft, porcelain skin of her ass. She turns, looking at me over her shoulder. The image almost does me in, almost makes me come on the spot.

"What are you waiting for?" she half whines, half moans. My girl is desperate for me. I can fucking smell it.

I remove my hands and then bring one down to smack her bare ass cheek, loving the way it jiggles and turns pink.

"Ah!" she yelps in surprise.

"That's for sassing me, Raven."

Her eyes go comically wide, and then squeeze shut. Raven arches her back, shoving herself closer to me, begging me for more. Again, I smack her juicy ass, and this time, she bucks her hips. One last spank, and then I massage the sting away. I slide a hand around her stomach and lower it into her folds.

Jesus Christ.

"You're so wet, Raven. Do you like being spanked? Like when I punish you?"

"I like ev-everything," she whimpers. God, my woman is so turned out it sounds painful.

I whip out my dick and tease her entrance, running the head up and down her seam, collecting her sweet honey. Grabbing her hips, I position myself at her entrance and slam into her. Hard.

Fucking hell.

Raven is always so tight, so hot and wet for me. It takes everything in me not to come the instant I'm inside of her. I pull out and slam into her again and again. She bucks her hips, meeting me thrust for thrust.

Her knuckles are white from how hard she's gripping the shelf in front of her. Books rattle around us, some even falling, but we don't stop. I love that she's so lost in us she doesn't even care that we're making a mess.

Golden light shimmers through the window, casting long shadows and highlighting Raven's curves, making her glow like the goddess she is.

My hands slide from her hips and grab her ass cheeks, pulling them apart so I can see her pussy stretch and take my cock. I keep rolling my hips, pounding into her as I feel my orgasm ready to rip through me.

I reach around and rub her clit, needing her to come first. Raven lets out a loud moan, and I nip the side of her neck.

"Quiet, Raven. We're in a library, after all."

I withdraw my fingers from her pussy and clap my hand over her mouth. She licks her juices off the palm of my hand, then bites the skin as she trembles and whimpers. I hook my other arm under her hips, holding her in place while I rut into her, barreling towards oblivion.

Pulling her earlobe between my teeth, I growl as I stroke in and out of her, deeper and deeper. "Come for me, beautiful Raven. I want to feel you come all over me."

I sink my teeth into her shoulder and she snaps, convulsing in my arms and shaking all over. Her pussy chokes my cock so fucking tight. I want to stay right here, on the edge of bliss, watching her spasm around my huge dick.

But I can't hang on another second. I thrust into her one last time and explode, painting her pussy walls with my sticky cum. I continue to pump into her, releasing more cum than I even knew I was capable of. Raven pulses around me again, my release triggering another orgasm inside of her.

Fuck.

She lets out a forceful breath that seems to drain the life out of her as she slumps against the half-empty bookshelf. I cover her with my body, wrapping her up in my arms. We're both sweaty and panting as we slowly come back down from our incredible shared high.

"Any other fantasies I should know about?" I whisper gruffly. Raven gives me a breathy laugh. I'll never get tired of that sound.

"I can hardly talk, let alone think," she says, turning her head to look at me over her shoulder.

"I fucked the words right out of you?" I tease. My girl giggles, and I spin her around in my arms, wrapping her up in a hug. "I love feeling your laughter when I hold you," I murmur, kissing the top of her head.

Raven tilts her face up, hitting me with those blue, green, and purple eyes. "Maybe I'm the one who fucked some words into you?" She scrunches her nose up at her own statement and then shakes her head no. "I told you I couldn't talk or think!" she says exasperatedly before snuggling against my chest.

"That's okay, baby girl. I have more to say if you want to just listen."

Raven pops her head up again, questions fluttering across her features. Nodding her head slowly, she raises an eyebrow, almost in challenge.

Shit. I didn't think this through. I was caught up in the moment, in her breathy moans and sparkling eyes.

"I… I have something. For you," I stutter out. "A question. And something else. I… fuck, I'm not saying it right," I mutter, taking a step back.

Raven places her hand on my chest, right over my heart. "I'm right here," she whispers. "I'll always be here."

How does she do that? Calm the storm with one touch?

"Would you like to make it official?" Raven gives me a questioning look. "Being here, being *mine* forever."

"Forever?"

"I'm messing this all up. You deserve to have flowers and rainbows and a fucking horseback ride at sunset," I ramble nervously. "Instead, you have me."

I gather her left hand from where it's resting on my chest. Lifting it up, I place a kiss on her ring finger and then take out the gold band I've been carrying around for the last week. Raven gasps, and I'm not sure if it's a good or bad sound.

I shove the ring on her finger as if once it's there, she has to accept her fate. Raven looks down at her hand, then back up at me, tears welling up in her eyes. Fuck, did I read this all wrong?

I'm about to step away and hide away in shame, but then Raven cups my cheeks, drawing my face down to meet hers. "Are you going to ask me?" she whispers, her breath tickling my lips.

Relief floods through me at her playful answer. "I'm not so good with words, remember?"

"Try."

Taking a deep breath, I press my lips to her hairline and then rest my forehead on hers. "Raven, you're the one bright spot in my dark, shadowed world. I was barely surviving before I met you. Then one look, one touch, and I knew I'd never be the same. Everything about you is soft, sweet, sassy, and perfect for me. I still don't believe I deserve your goodness in my life, but I'm trying real damn hard to live up to the man you think I am. The man you see in me."

"Slater..."

I cut her off with a chaste kiss. "I'm almost done," I say with a nervous grin. Raven smiles at me, her joy too great to be contained. Fuck, I'm glad she's so patient with me. "Will you marry me? Will you fill me up with your light every day for the rest of our lives? Will you let me love you and protect you and our kids with my dying breath?"

Tears wet Raven's cheeks, but she's still smiling at me, so that has to be good, right?

"Yes," she whispers. "Yes, yes, yes, yes, yes," Raven says over and over, peppering my face with kisses.

"Any other words you'd like to share?" I tease her, chuckling in between kisses. Raven shakes her head no and throws her arms around me. I pull her up and crush her against my chest, burying my face into the side of her neck. "I love you with everything in me," I whisper.

"You took the words right out of my mouth." Raven shakes with laughter and hold her closer, feeling the sweet sound travel through her body and into mine. This right here is more happiness than I ever knew was possible. I can't wait to have it every day for the rest of our lives.

Epilogue

Raven

"You like that, baby? Like when I fuck you rough and dirty?" he grits out, moving his hands to my hips and digging his fingers in. Slater bounces me off his cock, hitting home with each powerful stroke.

"Y-yes," I whimper, followed by a loud cry when he cracks his hand over my ass.

Slater grunts in satisfaction, then licks the sweat off the side of my neck, biting me there. I jerk my hips and clamp my pussy down on him, loving the pain he brings with my pleasure. I come so hard I can't take a full breath. I swear I can feel his cock all the way in my stomach.

Slater holds me up and pumps into me once, twice, three times, and then roars his own climax. His cum shoots into me in forceful bursts. We're both panting and sweating, trembling as our orgasms slowly fade. Every single time with Slater is amazing.

"Well, that's one way to christen the new house," Slater laughs as he scoops my limp body up in his arms and gets us settled on the couch, wrapping a blanket around our naked bodies.

"I would argue that it's the best way," I murmur, basking in the afterglow.

I feel more than hear the deep chuckle that bubbles out of his chest. Every single time he smiles or laughs, I feel like a powerful goddess. Slater has told me many times that there was no joy in his life before me. I don't know if that's true, but I'm blissfully happy knowing I can make the stoic giant laugh.

This last year has been crazy in the best way possible. Slater and I got married a month after he proposed. Our wedding was small, intimate, and perfect. Logan was there with his wife, Spencer, and of course, Colton and Shiloh were there as well.

I swear Colton's smile was going to rip his face in two the entire time. He insisted that we name our firstborn after him since he called our relationship early on. I don't know that we'll follow through on that suggestion, but it's something to think about. Especially with the news I have yet to share with my husband.

"What are you thinking about?" Slater whispers, stroking my back in calming circles.

I smile against his chest and turn my head to kiss him there. "Decorating our new home, of course," I reply.

"Oh yeah? And what are your plans, *krolik*?"

I push myself up a bit on his chest so we're eye-to-eye. God, his beautiful blue eyes get me every single time. I can't believe this incredibly sexy, rugged, perfect man is all mine. Forever.

"Raven?" he asks, a little smirk playing on his soft lips like he knows exactly what distracted me.

I bite my lip in an attempt to hold back my smile, but judging by the sparkle in his eyes, it didn't work. "I was thinking we'll need a sturdy four-poster bed, for obvious reasons."

Slater grins and nips at my jaw playfully. "What else?"

"Oh, you know. A crib, a bassinet, a changing table, and one of those comfy gliding rocker things for when the baby won't stop crying all night and you have to stay up with him or her. I'll need my beauty rest, of course," I wink at Slater.

His entire face is frozen in shock, almost as if his brain needs to catch up with what he just heard. "Crib? Baby?" he stutters out. He's completely adorable. I make a mental note to surprise him more often if he's going to give me cute, sexy looks like this.

I nod in confirmation. "And the rocking chair. Don't forget the rocking chair."

"For when I'm holding our baby," he says quietly, still a little dazed from the news.

"Yup. Our little baby that I'm growing in my belly right now. Little bean is about six weeks along."

"Oh my God, Raven," he whispers, his eyes growing glassy. "This is the best news. I can't... God, I'm so fucking happy," Slater says before cupping my face in his hands and pulling me forward so he can kiss me deeply. In one quick, yet careful move, he rolls us so I'm on my back on the couch. Slater kisses down my body and nuzzles into my belly, kissing me there. "You're mine. Both of you. I will love you with everything I am, protect you with everything that I have."

"You already do," I say kissing him lightly on the lips.

"Well, get ready for me to turn it up a notch. I'm talking overprotective, dedicated, obsessed husband here. You're going to be so pampered, like the goddess you are."

I laugh softly and look down at him. "You always make me feel that way."

"And I always will."

THE END

Also by Cameron Hart

Check out my other popular series and books!
Mafia, MC, & Bodyguard Romance:
<u>Moscatelli Crime Family Series</u>[1]
<u>Di Salvo Crime Family Series</u>[2]
<u>Chaos MC series</u>[3]
<u>Savage Ride</u>[4]
Mountain Man Romance:
<u>Men of Blackthorne Mountain Series</u>[5]
<u>Bear's Tooth Mountain Men Series</u>[6]
Cowboy & Small Town Romance:
<u>Roped in by Love Series</u>[7]

---

1. https://books2read.com/u/mqBaze

2. https://books2read.com/u/m0odzW

3. https://books2read.com/u/bMVAOk

4. https://books2read.com/u/bMVlG7

5. https://books2read.com/u/3RYDvB

6. https://books2read.com/u/mVel7A

7. https://books2read.com/u/3RYlBY